◇◇★◇◇

The Land Of Cotton

1861

Our Home in Dixieland

A Civil War Story Written by Ryana Lynn Miller

◇◇★◇◇

Historical Christian Fiction

The Land of Cotton

Ordering information:

Ryana Lynn Miller
1070 Cook Rd.
Denton, North Carolina 27239
Phone: (717) 873-8619
Email: lifeofheritage@gmail.com
Website: www.lifeofheritage.com

All Scriptures are taken from the KING JAMES BIBLE

Cover photo: Microsoft Word Clip Art

ISBN: 978-0-9863483-3-4

Printed in the United States of America

Historical Fiction

First Printing, January 2016
Second Printing, June 2016
Third Printing, August 2017
Fourth Printing, November 2018

★ 1861 ★

The Land of Cotton is dedicated to those who are willing to die if need be to defend their homes and their country! God Bless America! One Nation Under God, Sweet Land of Liberty!

★ 1861 ★

Contents

Acknowledgements

First, I would like to thank the Lord for His wisdom and guidance and for giving me the desire to write this book. Without Him, this book never would have been published. Thank You, Lord!

Next, I would like to thank my family for their encouragement, love and time spent on this project. Dad, thanks for personally proofing the sermon in this story! Mom, thanks for editing (and re-editing!) this book with me. I know there were a lot of other things you could have been doing! Your story plots, suggestions and comments helped to polish this book. And thank you for encouraging me to do more than just write for fun! I would like to thank my siblings, who have listened to me talk endlessly about this book for the past few years! Thank you for being both my critics and my encouragers. Your suggestions really helped a lot! Grandpa Miller, thank you so much for supplying a lot of my study material, proofing for grammatical errors, telling me more about your own study and for encouraging me all through this project. I appreciate it so much! I would like to thank my cousin Travis for using his knowledge of history and reenactment to check my book for historical accuracy. Thank you all!

Others I would like to thank are Bro. Beasley, for donating a laptop for me to type this book on and for encouraging me to publish this book; Bro. Tim for taking time to help with proofing; and Bro. Randy for donating part of his Civil War book collection to me! Two books in particular helped a lot with my research and saved me a lot of time!

Lastly, thanks to all of you who have prayed for me, encouraged me and listened to me while preparing this book for printing. You'll never know how much you've helped me!

Introduction

The Mason Family is based on Southerners of the 1860's and events that *could* have happened. Cotton farming was a common enterprise during this time. As much as this may surprise you, it was not uncommon for Southerners to be abolitionists, or just not own slaves. I believe slavery is wrong, but this book is *NOT* about slavery. This book is about the factual cause of the War Between the States.

The use of the words Yankee, Yank, Bullies, Rebel and Reb is not used to offend anyone, but to keep the story realistic.

To help clarify which characters and important events are historic and which are fictional, footnotes have been placed at the bottom of the pages.

Since the word dinner can mean lunch or supper, depending on where you're from, I will clarify that in this book it means lunch.

Also, Washington D.C. in those days was known as Washington City or just Washington.

So, here is *"The Land of Cotton!"* Enjoy and God Bless!

In Christ, Ryana Lynn

★ 1861 ★

Characters of Importance

The Southerners

The Mason Family: Silas owns the Shady Grove Cotton Plantation. He and his wife, Ellen, have four children: Richard (18), Seth (16), Dixianna (15) and Michael (12).

◇◇★◇◇

Mr. and Mrs. Bradley: Leonard and Eva Bradley have worked at Shady Grove as long as the Mason children can remember. Mr. Bradley is Silas' right hand man, while Mrs. Bradley is the family cook and housekeeper.

◇◇★◇◇

Lana Brewster (17): Pastor Brewster's daughter and close friend of Dixie's. She loves children and often assists the local midwife.

◇◇★◇◇

Tyler Nace (16): Lana's cousin on her father's side.

◇◇★◇◇

Jeremiah "Jeremy" Calling (17): A young man originally from Maryland who has joined the Confederate Army.

◇◇★◇◇

Cpl. Titus Mallory (19): A soldier under General Jackson.

◇◇★◇◇

Pvt. Nate Bowers (13): A Confederate drummer boy.

◇◇★◇◇

David Bowers: Older brother to Nate. He is a doctor's aide in the Confederate Army.

◇◇★◇◇

The Roberts Family: Will and Lou are free blacks and have three children and one on the way. Their children are Reuben (12), Salina May (8), and Troy (4).

◇◇★◇◇

<u>Papa and Nana Rains:</u> Ellen's parents, from Philadelphia.

◇◇★◇◇

<u>Main Northern Cousins:</u> Philip Rains (20), Jennifer Rains (16), Andrew "Drew" Cameron (17), Allison Cameron (15), and Constance Angelica Tinderman, (16).

◇◇★◇◇

<u>Pvt. Rodney Badin Jr.:</u> Typical bully. The Masons become acquainted with him in an undesirable manner.

◇◇★◇◇

<u>Pvt. Evans:</u> A Yankee soldier whom the Masons encounter more than once. He's the "Kind Yankee."

...And they shall fight every one against his brother, and every one against his neighbor; city against city, and kingdom against kingdom.

Isaiah 19:2b

"Trusting in Almighty God, an approving conscience, and the aid of my fellow-citizens, I devote myself to the service of my native State, in whose behalf alone will I ever again draw my sword."

Robert Edward Lee, April 23rd, 1861

Chapter 1

"How'd This All Get Started?"

*T*ap, tap, tap, t-t-t, tap, tap, tap.

"Mason, you got that one?"

"Yes, Mr. Burton. It's addressed to the sheriff."

"Deliver it before you go home for the day."

"Yes, sir."

Seth Mason, sixteen, worked at a telegraph/newspaper office in Four Tree Springs, North Carolina. It was January 11, 1861, and Seth was depressed. Being a telegraph operator, he knew what news he was giving to the sheriff. Alabama had seceded.

"This is the third secession this week," he exclaimed. "Last year it was just South Carolina, and now it's Mississippi, Florida and Alabama. This is craziness!"

Seth made his way over to the sheriff's house to deliver his telegram. He knocked on the door. As he waited for the sheriff to open the door, Seth wondered if the sheriff would be saddened by the message. It seemed their country was heading for ruin.

Finally, the door opened and Seth handed him the message. He was given a tip for delivery and an invitation to come in out of the wind for a moment.

Sheriff Gallimore wasn't upset by the note. He was an avid secessionist and eager for North Carolina to join the 'Brave leading states of Southern beliefs.' Seth figured Sheriff Gallimore would fight, if necessary, to retain what he held dear to him.

Seth's family felt the same way. Seth agreed that the South was right, but he thought there was a better way to handle things. Why couldn't they talk things out? Some felt war was in the near future, especially since South Carolina had fired on a U.S. ship two days before.[1]

Seth pulled his coat tighter against the chill coming down from the mountain as he left the sheriff's house. He urged his father's horse, Charger, into a fast trot toward the general store. His eighteen year old brother, Richard, worked there and they got off work about the same time. As he approached the store, Richard walked out, bundled up against the wind. Seth waved a greeting as Richard mounted his horse, Champion.

"Hey, Seth, is there any noteworthy news?"

Seth frowned. "Just secession, that's all. It's Alabama this time. Next thing you know, Arkansas, Georgia, Texas, and

---

[1] On January 9th, 1861, the U.S. ship *Star of the West*, was fired upon by South Carolinians. The ship was on its way to Ft. Sumter with men and supplies to hold the fort. They were turned back and the men already there had to hold the fort alone.

who knows who else will secede. Then people will be fighting their cousins in their own backyards!"

Richard listened to Seth with interest. "I suspect you're right. War could be just around the corner. But things could change. Just because four states left the Union doesn't mean the Yanks will take up arms against them."

"True, but everyone knows them Yankees. They'll push it 'til others leave. Then someone's temper will flare up and BANG! We're right in the middle of a war!" Seth shook his head at the thought.

Richard nodded thoughtfully, "Maybe so."

★ 1861 ★

Bang!

Dixianna jumped in her seat. Seth and Richard walked into the kitchen where their fourteen year old sister sat peeling potatoes. "How many times do me and Mama have to tell y'all not to slam the front door? You almost made me cut my finger!"

Her words suggested that she was upset, but Dixie grinned at her brothers. Even though she had three brothers, two older and one younger, Dixie still wasn't used to the slamming of doors.

Michael, twelve, sat next to his sister working on his homework. He couldn't help but laugh at Dixie's jumpiness.

"Sorry, Dixie," Seth apologized, removing his hat and smoothing down his blonde hair. Then turning to his younger brother he asked, "How was school today, Michael?"

"Good," he said, tapping his pencil on the table, "I did okay on that English paper. I got 100%! And I have to make a bunch of visits to Dr. Wilmore's office for my paper on medicines and their uses."

"How long is that paper supposed to be?" Seth asked.

Michael ran his fingers through his dark brown hair. "About…hmm…5 to 6 pages."

Seth was surprised. He had never written a paper that long when he was in Michael's grade.

"Didn't you just write a paper for school?" added Richard.

"Last week I wrote a shorter one on the Mexican War, and Mr. Pierce thought I should try a topic other than history. It's an extensive topic though. Dixie said she'd help me get the right kinds of information from Dr. Wilmore. "

Richard grinned. "She'd be the one to ask. Hey, Seth, don't you have a book about that stuff in your collection?"

Seth thought for a moment. "No, I borrowed that one from Dr. Wilmore." Seth was saving his money to enroll in medical school in the near future. Dixie had picked up her interest in medicine from her brother's contagious enthusiasm.

Richard and Seth helped with the family cotton plantation and their jobs in town became part-time jobs during cotton season.

Richard, looking around, asked, "Where is everybody?"

Dixie smiled mischievously as she put some potato peelings in the scrap bucket. "Let's see…Papa's with Pastor Brewster, inviting people in Parkersburg to the camp meeting. Mama's at the Shayne's house, delivering their baby, because midwife Faber's out of town. I'm fixing supper, Michael's working on his homework, you're milking Bet, and Seth is throwing out these potato peelings to the hogs."

"Okay, little sister," Richard said to Dixie as he pulled Seth toward the door. "We can take a hint." Laughing, they went to perform their assigned tasks. Michael snickered and got back to his schoolwork. Dixie returned to her supper preparations.

Dixie had done meals by herself before, but she was having trouble concentrating on this one. Normally Mrs. Bradley did the cooking, as she was the family's cook. But today Mr. and Mrs. Bradley were out of town.

As she prepared to fry the potatoes, she thought over her mother's instructions. *I need to fry the potatoes, onions, and tenderloin. Then make the gravy. I've already made the biscuits and sweet tea. So it looks like everything will be ready on time.*

★ 1861 ★

14

"Pass the biscuits!"

"How's Mrs. Shayne?"

"How was work, Richard?"

"Was the baby a boy or a girl?"

"Did anyone say they would come to the meetings?"

"Pass the fried taters!"

"Shhh! Everyone stop for a minute!" exclaimed Papa. "Dixie, pass Seth the biscuits, and Richard, pass the taters to Michael. Let's try not to talk all at once," he reproved gently. He turned to his wife Ellen. "How's Mrs. Shayne and the baby?"

"They're both fine. Miss Faber got there just after the baby came. It's a girl! They named her Olivia. She's adorable. She's got blonde hair and the darkest blue eyes I've ever seen. Looks just like her mother's side of the family. And speaking of them, her parents were there. Mrs. Burton even assisted me in the delivery. The boys were so excited to have a little sister."

"Finally, a girl!" Dixie said excitedly. "The last three babies that have been born around here have been boys."

Richard spoke up next. "Papa, how many people said they were coming to the camp meeting?"

Papa buttered his biscuit as he answered, "Well, we visited ten families, and most seemed interested. Pastor Brewster said that little town has finally built a church of their own. Now they're waiting on a preacher. 'Til then, I guess they'll keep coming to our church."

"That's great!" Richard replied. "Are the Tanners coming?" he asked hopefully, for he had been witnessing to Mr. Tanner and his oldest son Brandon for a long time.

Papa shook his head. "No. Mr. Tanner is a stubborn man. And Brandon is just like him. I'm afraid God will have to do something big to get their attention."

Richard sighed, "I sure hope not, but you're probably right."

"It must be hard for Mrs. Tanner with her husband not coming to church with her and the children," Mama commented. "And she's been sick lately, too."

"It is sad. We need to pray for them more," replied Papa.

"Why don't we pray for them right now?" Richard requested.

"Go ahead, son," Papa suggested. And pray he did, begging God to save Mr. Tanner and Brandon and praying for strength for Mrs. Tanner and the rest of the children.

"Thank you, Richard. Oh, Seth, any news today?" his father asked.

Seth grew despondent. "Alabama seceded. We're getting closer to out and out war everyday it seems." Michael squirmed in his seat. He was excited about all this, but he didn't want to upset his brother by showing it.

Seth glanced at his twelve year old brother and smiled. "Michael, I'm not against what's going on, I just wish there was a better way to get our point across. In some ways, I'm just as excited as you. But when I think about the possibilities of a lot of people dying, I wish there was another way. But," he sighed, "I guess I'm just repeating myself."

Dixie spoke up. "That doesn't matter. Lots of people repeat themselves to get an important point across. And I think yours is important."

"I do too," Papa said gravely. "There's nothing glamorous about the battlefield. Families turn on each other, souls go out into eternity, and some burn forever in hell. War is a serious matter, children. We don't need to take it lightly."

The children knew he was thinking about his uncle who had died in the war with Mexico. He and Uncle Thomas were about the same age and had enlisted together.

"Papa, why can't all this be settled peaceably? How'd this all get started?" Michael questioned.

"Well son, there's always been differences between the North and the South- cultural differences. The North tries to find ways to make work easier and faster, so they can make more money with less work. We, on the other hand, do things the way we've been doing them for generations.

"For years, the North has used the South's productiveness to benefit them. I remember my Papa telling me that he used to sell cotton to northern contractors and they wouldn't pay him enough to make any profit. One year he barely had enough to cover expenses. Then, the Yankees in return would make material and other things out of our cotton and sell it to us for outrageous prices. So, like other plantation owners, Papa took a contract with an Englishman. The English paid honest wages and Papa was able to make a decent living.

"Well, the Yanks didn't like it that most of our cotton was going overseas. They were having to buy materials from England to make their goods and they weren't making all that extra profit like they used to. We worked hard for the money we made and simply wanted to be paid what our materials and labor were worth. But the government raised taxes on imported and exported goods. The tax was supposed to 'protect' the Yankee factories by making it too expensive for us to trade outside of the U.S. They resorted to taxes rather than going out and working harder themselves or paying us decent wages.

"That was about forty years ago, back in the twenties and thirties when I was growing up. South Carolina threatened to secede then and almost did, but they got things worked out temporarily. They kept taxing us unjustly, though.

"Another thing that counts into the present state of things is that the North tries to change our way of life, saying we need to use factories instead of good old-fashioned, hard work. We don't want to change and have no reason to. They keep trying, and we keep refusing. They have no right to force us, and we know it. The North is mad 'cause we won't change, and we're mad because they won't leave us alone. So now, the states have started seceding to protect their rights from being taken away."

The others nodded in agreement. Papa continued, "It would take a lifetime to tell you everything, I just scratched the surface."

"If you just scratched the surface, I don't want to dig deeper!" declared Michael. Everyone laughed.

"Michael, you might change your mind," replied Papa. "You need to know why the South is fighting against the North in politics, in newspapers, in books, in schoolrooms, in word, and maybe even someday, in combat. It's important that you understand it. Do you remember those Revolutionary War stories we tell?"

Michael nodded. "Good," continued Papa. "Well, think of it this way, the North are the British and we are the Patriots. That's the way it is. We are trying to gain our independence from Yankee tyranny."

Though this conversation had been between Papa and Michael, everyone had listened intently. Everyone understood that Mr. Mason wasn't trying to turn his family against the north. As a matter of fact, Mrs. Mason was born and raised in Pennsylvania. Everyone on her side of the family lived in the north.

The rest of the meal was more pleasant. Richard informed the family that the prices of sewing supplies had gone down by 25%. Michael relayed a story from school about the Shayne's chickens getting loose and the boys chasing them. They finally caught them and found they had caught three chickens too many! The Lanier family was glad to get their stray chickens back.

Afterward, Richard and Seth went out to do the evening chores while Dixie and Michael cleaned up the kitchen. Silas and Ellen were discussing things concerning the family cotton business.

When the children were finished with their chores, they met in the back parlor to play some music. Richard brought in his guitar and Seth tuned up his mandolin. Dixie rosined the bow for her fiddle and Michael played his harmonica. They played hymns and folk songs and had a good time. Later, they all gathered for family devotions, and soon everyone was heading for bed.

★1861★

Chapter 2

★

The Move

Rejoice evermore. Pray without ceasing. In every thing give thanks:
for this is the will of God in Christ Jesus concerning you.
I Thessalonians 5:16-18

"Class is dismissed." The students of Mt. Dogwood schoolhouse grabbed papers and books and tried to remember their assignments. Dixie finished helping Mr. Pierce grade papers and then met Michael outside the schoolhouse. The two headed toward the doctor's clinic in the middle of town. With just a little more information, Michael's paper would be ready.

A week had passed since their talk around the kitchen table, and the weather was much warmer.

"Dixie! Dixianna Mason, hold up!" The Mason siblings turned and saw Dixie's seventeen year old friend, Lana Brewster, rushing toward them.

Lana was an only child and Pastor Brewster was her only living parent, her mother having died of scarlet fever when Lana was five. Lana considered Dixie as the sister she never had.

"Guess what?" Lana nearly shouted.

Dixie grinned. "With you, it could be anything! What?"

19

"Guess!"

"You've just found out that your horse, Rose, is gonna have a baby?"

"No, guess again!"

"Well…"

"My cousins are moving here today! They're moving here, to Four Tree Springs! I'm so excited! Papa told me this morning, and I've been waiting for school to let out so I could tell you!"

Dixie's eyes widened. "They're moving here today? Isn't that sorta short notice?"

Lana nodded. "Yes, but their letter was delayed, and they were also able to leave a little earlier than expected."

"That's great! So which cousins are these?"

"My papa's sister's family."

Dixie laughed. "Lana, your papa has three sisters!"

"Oh…yeah! It's my Aunt Kathie and Uncle Jonathan Nace. You've never met them."

"Lana! I'm so happy for you! I can't wait to meet them. How many children do they have?"

"They have four. Let's see…Tyler's close to Seth's age. Then there's Annie, Carter, and Alyssa Rose."

"So, what's their reason for moving here? Where are they from?" Dixie asked.

"They've been in Baltimore, Maryland for a long time and Uncle Jonathan believes it's time to get his children away from the city. They're originally from Mississippi like us.

"Uncle Jonathan is in the indigo business, and it just hasn't been going well in Baltimore," Lana continued. "And with all the unrest lately, they really want to get back south."

Dixie smiled as she looked at her friend. Lana's blonde hair was wavy and her gray eyes always seemed to sparkle. Dixie always enjoyed her company. The two friends were very contrasting in looks. Dixie's hair was bright red and quite curly. It was hard to manage at times, but she loved her curls. Her eyes were emerald green.

All this time, the three had been walking. They passed the telegraph office, and Dixie waved at Seth through the window. Her brother grinned and waved back.

"Where are you headed, Dixie?" Lana asked after a moment.

"Oh, I'm going to the general store, then to Dr. Wilmore's clinic to help Michael with his paper. Want to come with us? It shouldn't take too long."

"Sure, that sounds like fun!"

Michael asked to wait outside, as the store could be somewhat stuffy and he was already sort of hot from playing around at the school grounds. Richard, as usual, was running the counter. Dixie had some things to pick up for her mother. "Hey, Richard," she greeted as she entered the store.

"Hey, Dixie. Hey, Lana. What can I do for y'all today?"

Dixie fished her list out of her hand bag. "Let's see…we need some flour, sugar and baking soda. Mrs. Bradley said she wants you to bring it home after work. She needs the flour before supper. I have to go to Dr. Wilmore's office with Michael, and you'll get home before I will."

"No problem." Richard wrote up the bill, and Dixie gave him the money. She walked over to the material racks while Richard filled an order for Lana.

A soft purple cotton material caught her eye. It was beautiful. Lana stepped up next to her. "That would make a nice dress with this lace around the collar, sleeves and hem," she said as she picked up a deep shade of purple lace and held it against the fabric.

"Yes, it would. That's really pretty," Dixie agreed.

Lana fingered it gently. Her eyes lit up as she thought of an idea. "Hey, you know that brown dress on the cover of that fashion book your cousin sent you for Christmas? We said it looked too plain and simple for Yankee ladies. Remember?"

Dixie nodded. "Yeah, I remember it. What about it?"

"That would be a pretty pattern to use with this material," Lana explained.

"Yes, it would. I really like the color."

Later, the girls and Michael arrived at Dr. Wilmore's office. It was rather small because the back part of the office was the Wilmores' home.

The clinic smelled of dried herbs, medicines, and lye soap. Dr. Wilmore soon arrived and answered all of Michael's questions. After thanking the grandfatherly man for his help, they left the office.

★ 1861 ★

While the young people were at the doctor's office, Silas Mason had gone over to the Pastor's house to assess some repairs that were needing to be done to the barn. They, too, had talked of the Nace family's move to Four Tree Springs. "Silas, I was wondering if you would mind your boys spending some time with Tyler. He's a good young man, very mild tempered. But Jonathan wrote in his letter that Tyler has become very quiet and withdrawn lately. Jonathan's hoping that moving away from the city will remedy the situation."

Silas nodded as he stopped writing notes to think about what the Pastor was saying. "So what's odd about a boy going through a quiet stage? Seth's usually quiet, but I've not been concerned about it."

Pastor Brewster paused from moving some boards. "Of course, that's Seth's nature to be on the quiet side, but Tyler's generally outgoing and now he's distanced himself from people."

"It's these troubled times we live in," Silas said, shaking his head. "It's already begun to wreak its havoc on our young people. Perhaps the move will do them all some good."

★ 1861 ★

"Mama, Mama!" Michael called as he bolted in the front door. He rushed to the kitchen where Mama was helping Mrs. Bradley prepare supper. "Guess what! Lana's Uncle and Aunt, the Naces, are moving here! Today! And they have four children!"

"Slow down, boy! Who's moving in today?" Mama asked, pulling a chocolate cake from the oven. Mrs. Bradley smiled at the youngster as she stirred the stew they were having for supper. Dixie joined them at that moment and filled the ladies in on the Nace family.

"Lana wants me to go with her to the depot when they get here," Dixie continued. "May I go, please?"

"I think that would be fine. Michael, I'd let you go too, but you've got homework to do and I don't think it will wait."

Michael nodded, "Yes, ma'am. I'll get right to it."

"Ellen!" Silas called out, entering the back door. "Pastor Brewster just told me that his sister Kathie Nace and her family are moving here today. Do we have enough food fixed to have them and the Brewsters over for supper? That's eight extra people."

Mama turned a questioning gaze towards Mrs. Bradley. The elder lady answered for her, "Of course, I made a stew for tonight, and we've got plenty!"

"I'd like to have them over," Mama agreed. "That will give Michael an incentive to finish his homework quickly," she said, smiling at her youngest son.

"Great," Papa answered. Then thinking of something, he called for Richard.

Richard poked his head into the kitchen. "Yes, sir?"

"Go with Dixie to the Brewsters and tell Pastor that when his family gets here, we'll have supper ready, if they don't have anything planned."

"Yes, sir." He reached over Dixie's head to get his hat. Then he paused. "He's got family moving here today?"

"Yes," Dixie said, hurrying him out the door. "I'll fill you in on the way." Soon they arrived at the Brewsters' out of breath. The Brewsters lived right inside town, but it was still only a few minutes from the Masons' plantation. Dixie knocked on the door and Lana opened it.

"Dixie, your face is so red! Did you run here? Come inside. Oh, hey Richard."

"Hey, Lana. Is your father here?"

"Yes, come on in." She led them to the sitting room. Pastor Brewster stood and greeted them with a smile as they entered.

"Hey, Pastor. How are you?" Richard said, shaking hands with him.

"Very well, thank you, Richard. How about y'all?" Pastor Brewster asked, glancing at Dixie, who was still panting.

"We're fine," Richard said, grinning at his sister. "Papa and Mama want you, Lana and your sister's family to come to our house for supper tonight, if you don't already have plans. Is that alright, Pastor?"

"Yes, of course! That sounds great!"

"What time do they get here?" Dixie asked as the girls reached Lana's room.

"In about ten minutes. Um, you might want to redo your hair, Dixie. Look in the mirror."

She looked and laughed again. "I guess loops and fly-aways wouldn't look good at the depot." She quickly fixed her hair. The light coming through the window made her silky, copper curls shine.

Soon Pastor Brewster was knocking on Lana's door. "Y'all want to go with us and wait at the depot instead of staying here a few more minutes?"

"Sure, let's!" Lana exclaimed. So off to the depot they went.

★ 1861 ★

The train pulled into the depot. Lana quickly scanned the cars and platform, which were full of people and luggage. "They're getting off of car four!" Lana pointed. "That's them!" The group hurried over to the family.

"Uncle Jonathan! Aunt Kathie!"

"Lana! It's so good to see you! Jonathan, look who's here to meet us!" Aunt Kathie was very friendly and Dixie liked her instantly.

Uncle Jonathan hugged his niece as Pastor Brewster walked up to greet his sister and brother-in-law. "And who are these young people with y'all today, Andrew?"

"These are two of my church members, Jonathan. This is Richard Mason. And this is his sister Dixianna, but everybody calls her Dixie. Their family is providing our supper tonight."

"How very nice of them," Aunt Kathie said, smiling at Dixie.

Pastor Brewster glanced around. "Where's Tyler?"

"I'm here, Uncle Andrew," Tyler said, coming around his parents. He was holding Alyssa Rose, who'd fallen asleep. Richard studied the young man's face. He looked tired and serious.

He shook hands with his uncle as he balanced his little sister in his arms. Tyler glanced at Richard and then looked down. Richard introduced himself and tried to initiate some small talk. Carter stood next to them, smiling up at Richard. Richard immediately shook hands with the younger brother, and guessing he was around Michael's age, he told him all about Michael.

A girl with dark blonde hair stepped up next to Dixie. "I'm Annie. I've heard a lot about you, Dixie, in Lana's letters. She's already told me that we have the same birthday. I'm glad I finally get to meet you."

"It's good to meet you too. Welcome to Four Tree Springs."

The group headed to the Brewsters' house first to drop off trunks, and then went to Shady Grove, the Masons' plantation, for supper. Dixie, Lana, Annie and Alyssa Rose spent the evening around the piano together, while Michael and Carter talked about fishing…and their common interests in the possibility of a war. Richard, Seth and Tyler talked in the parlor with the adults. The boys had their work cut out for them trying to keep Tyler in the conversation, but persistence paid off and he began to contribute after a while. Aunt Kathie smiled. It was good to see Tyler talking to other young men again.

Yes, the Masons really liked the Nace Family. They would fit in just fine.

 ★1861★

Chapter 3

★

Agree to Disagree

If it be possible, as much as lieth in you, live peaceably with all men.
Romans 12:18

◇◇★◇◇

"But what a cruel thing is war; to separate and destroy families and
friends, and mar the purest joys and happiness
God has granted us in this world; ..."
Robert E. Lee

T he Nace family did fit in just fine. They bought a house in town and made preparations to start their indigo business. Their oldest son, Tyler, got a job at Mr. Burton's telegraph/newspaper office as a typesetter. Annie and Carter went to the school, and the family became active workers in the church.

The Davidson County Camp Meeting went well. Souls were saved and hearts were revived. Dutiful Mrs. Tanner came every night despite her ill health. Her younger children came with her, but Mr. Tanner and their older son Brandon stayed behind.

The church had special prayer for lost loved ones every night. Mr. Tanner and Brandon were among the names on that list.

Many things were happening in the political world as well. On the 19th of January, Georgia seceded. That same day, Virginia suggested that a national peace conference be held to "mend the rift between the North and South."

On the 26th of January, Louisiana seceded. Three days later on the 29th, Kansas was admitted into the Union as the thirty-fourth state.

Then on the first of February, Texas seceded. On the 4th, Virginia's peace conference became a reality in Washington City. The seceded states held a meeting of their own that day, in Alabama, to organize their new government. On the 8th of February, they adopted their constitution for "The Confederate States of America," as they called themselves.

The next day, February 9th, President Jefferson Davis[2] and Vice-President Alexander Stephens[3] were elected by the new country.

★ 1861 ★

"War's getting a grip on the states, ain't it, Papa?" asked Michael at supper. "Everybody's mad at everybody else!" Although Dixie laughed a little under her breath, the idea of war really frightened her.

Papa nodded. "Yes, Michael, war is coming, and everyone's upset about it. Unless a miracle happens, we'll be fighting by this summer."

---

[2] The 1st and only President of the Confederate States of America. Davis did not, at first, want the presidency, but later served in his office with vigor and passion for freedom.
[3] The 1st and only Vice-President of the Confederate States of America.

Dixie shuddered. Richard looked at her and grinned. "Dixie, with all your medical know-how, the Confederates and Yankees will be fighting over you!"

"And I'll tell them that the South wins!" Everyone laughed. More seriously, she added, "They'd better fight over Lana. She knows much more than I do. She's assisted Miss Faber in delivering babies, she's helped in Dr. Wilmore's clinic when needed, and who knows what else."

After a brief silence, Papa said, "Children, how would y'all like to visit Papa and Nana Rains in Philadelphia?"

"Could we? What about my school?" Michael asked excitedly.

"Well, Mr. Pierce agreed to help you double up in your school this week, so we can leave this Saturday and come back next Saturday."

Cheers erupted from the table. Then Richard asked, "What's the reason for this trip? We don't usually rush up there at a moment's notice. Is everyone alright?" He was fearful that maybe his grandparents were sick.

Papa looked at Mama. "Well, Papa Rains has called for a family meeting concerning the secessions and the prospect of war. He wrote that he knew war was coming and that some of your cousins were gonna enlist as soon as war breaks out. He said he was sure the subject had been discussed here."

Richard ran his fingers through his reddish brown hair and winced. Seth looked down at his plate. Seth knew how his grandfather felt about the possibility of war. Papa Rains had said in a letter once that the "secessionists should be brought back to the Union and their leaders tried for treason."

Seth also knew how he himself felt about the matter. Even at the age of sixteen, he had peace with God that if it did come to war, and if his parents consented, he would join the Confederacy…someday.

This conclusion had not come easy for him. As a child, he had thought he would never go to war and have mother worrying over him like she did for Papa. But the firm belief that the south was indeed struggling to gain its independence, and many sleepless nights spent in prayer had made the decision for him.

Papa picked up the letter lying next to his plate. The rustle of the pages brought Seth back from his thoughts. "It says here, 'Your presence at this family gathering is greatly requested. Your last visit was far too long ago. We are also paying to have a family photograph taken, just in case. It wouldn't do to leave part of the family out.'"

The family knew what "just in case" was implying. Silas gave Ellen a side-glance. Tears were filling her eyes. How well he remembered her reaction to the letter when they had first read it together.

Ellen had mixed feelings about the whole issue. After all, she was Philadelphian born; her side of the family all lived in the north.

She loved her family, and truth be told, she loved the Union. The states were stronger united; she knew that, and Silas knew that. It hadn't been that long ago that he'd served in the army. And now this.

Silas completely understood how Ellen felt. This was her family they were talking about. Those were her nephews mentioned in the letter, not just some random soldier. The very idea that someday they could be fighting against her husband or sons or both made her sick.

She felt so torn. Her family clung firmly to the Union; her husband's family clung firmly to the cause of freedom. The couple had talked and prayed long into the night on many a night. They had to make the decision for *their* family…not Ellen's family or Silas'…*their* family.

In the end, they had sided with the South. If North Carolina remained in the Union, they would move farther south. If she seceded, they would fully support their state's decision. Many tears had been shed over this subject, but Ellen stood loyally by her husband, and she could honestly say she trusted his decision for their family.

Papa folded the letter and placed it back in the envelope. Mama dabbed her eyes with her napkin. She managed to smile at her husband. He took her hand as he turned toward the family. "We will have to explain to Papa Rains that we agree with the Confederate views. This conflict isn't easy for me or your mother; even though we disagree with Papa Rains, he is still part of our family. Let us be praying. We don't want the family to split over this problem."

Mama nodded in agreement. A split was the last thing she wanted to happen. Things were hard enough without that happening!

★1861★

"Dixie, it's time to get up. Can you hear me?" Dixie woke up as Seth began to knock on her door. "Dixie, are you up yet?"

"Yes, I'm awake now," she answered sleepily. Dixie quickly got ready for the day, headed down the winding steps, and then to the dining room.

"Happy birthday, Dixie!" everyone shouted as she entered the room. Dixie stared in amusement at the "decorations." The boys had drawn pictures and hung them from the ceiling. Dixie had never known her brothers to be artists, but these pictures were beautiful. They depicted different things the boys had done with her during the past year.

She gave each of her family members a hug. One of the pictures caught her eye and upon closer observation, she recognized herself falling into the pond on their property, and Seth, the "knight in shining armor," pulling her out onto the bank. She wrinkled her nose at her sixteen year old brother, and he smirked.

"I told you I'd never let you live that down!" Seth whispered as she grinned and elbowed him.

Richard laughed and said, "Fifteen! Dixie, you're getting old!"

"Well if I'm old, then you're ancient," returned Dixie, as the family gathered around the table for breakfast.

Mrs. Bradley had outdone herself with Dixie's favorites: eggs, bacon, and apple turnovers. After breakfast, the boys gave Dixie a gift. They had bought the material, lace and pattern she and Lana had discussed in the store the month before.

Dixie was delighted. "Richard, were you listening when me and Lana were talking about this?"

Richard smiled sheepishly. "Yes, and Mama was a big help too."

Dixie gave each brother a hug. "Thank y'all so much. I can't wait to work on it!" The boys smiled. They were satisfied that their money was well spent.

Papa handed her another package. She opened it and inside was the prettiest leather covered journal Dixie had ever seen. *Dixianna* was pressed elegantly on the cover. "Oh! Papa, Mama, it's so beautiful! Thank y'all!"

"You're welcome," Mama replied. "I'm glad you like it."

"Michael has a separate gift for you as well," Papa said.

Michael bit his lip as he handed Dixie the gift. She opened the box and withdrew a homemade horse halter and bridle set. Dixie was a bit puzzled by the unusual gift, but she liked it just the same.

"Michael! Did you make these?" He nodded. "They're very well made! Thank you! Who taught you to work the leather and metal?"

"Paw-Paw Mason did. He got me started on it when I went to visit them last fall. It was fun, but I really didn't know what to do with it once I made it. Papa suggested I give it to you."

Papa spoke up. "I suppose I should explain." His eyes twinkled, and he turned to Dixie. All eyes were on Papa. "There was another topic of interest in that last letter from your Papa Rains. He sent the money for you and Seth to each buy a horse."

Dixie's eyes danced with excitement. "Really Papa? My very own horse?"

"Yes, your very own. There's to be a horse sale this April. Find the ones y'all want, and they're yours."

Seth had known about this gift, but Dixie, of course, had not. She was speechless. Suddenly, the school bell began to ring out. Dixie and Michael raced to get their coats. They said good-bye and ran toward the schoolhouse. Dixie helped out at the school on Mondays and Thursdays and would not want to set a bad example by being late.

Mama laughed as they disappeared down the hill. "I believe they'll be there on time, don't you?" she asked her husband.

"Yes, I believe they will," Papa replied.

★ 1861 ★

The train swayed and lurched. Dixie closed her eyes. *Don't get sick,* she thought. *Whatever you do, DO NOT get sick!* She still wasn't used to riding in a train car, and she hadn't felt her best the day they left for Philadelphia. She prayed, pleading with God not to let her get sick. Michael wasn't feeling his best either.

Seth was sitting next to her, absorbed in a small volume. "What are you reading?" she asked.

"*Law; or Basic Notes for the Aspiring Lawyer,*" was the response. "I borrowed it from Sheriff Gallimore."

Dixie glanced at her brother, somewhat puzzled. "I thought you wanted to be a doctor."

"I do," he sighed and then went on to explain, "I'm just tired of visiting up in Philadelphia and not understanding what cousin Charles is talking about." Charles was a law student and used big words no one understood.

Dixie giggled. "Seth, I know it's hard to get all of what he says, but it ain't that bad! He can't help the fact that he's a northerner, plus a college student. What are you gonna do? Walk around with that law book and when you hear a word you don't understand, look it up?"

"No, but I would like to understand him a little bit better."

Dixie's thoughts turned toward her northern family members. Her mother had one brother and three sisters and several nieces and nephews. When they got together, it was hard to keep straight who was a Rains, Tinderman, Cameron, Mason or Culwright! Dixie couldn't wait to see Allison Cameron. They were very close and since they both had red hair and green eyes, many people mistook them for twins. They didn't mind a bit!

It was a good thing the Rains Estate had a very large house and guest house. In fact, Uncle Robert Rains' family and Uncle Charles Tinderman's family lived there, since both of the men helped run the family railroad equipment factories.

Uncle Charles helped with out of town business and Uncle Robert ran the office, that way Papa Rains could relax in his aging years. Plus, Papa and Nana loved having family close by. And there was plenty of room for company.

The Masons and Camerons usually stayed at the home place, but the Culwrights stayed in the family guest house, so as not to crowd things too much.

Dixie finished reminiscing just as the train pulled into the station.

"Philadelphia!" shouted the Conductor. As they stepped off the train, Dixie prayed once more about Mama and Papa having to explain things to Papa Rains.

After getting their bags, the Masons noticed a tall, medium built young man approaching them. Michael didn't recognize him, but the others did. "Philip! It's so good to see you!" Ellen said, giving her nephew a hug.

So this is Philip, thought Michael. *He sure has changed.* The Masons hadn't seen Philip Rains in three years due to various reasons, and he looked quite different than what Michael remembered, or maybe it was just the mustache.

"Grandfather sent me with the carriage to pick you all up. Right this way," he said, taking his Aunt's bag.

"His manners haven't changed," Dixie whispered to Michael. "He's still as gentlemanly as ever."

"Yep, sure is."

★ 1861 ★

Philip wasn't the only one who hadn't changed. Once they reached Papa and Nana Rains' house, Dixie realized that

Constance Angelica Tinderman was just as moody as she remembered. She took one look at Dixie and gasped, fanning herself as though she might faint. "The very idea of wearing white in the dead of winter!"

Dixie looked at Richard with a puzzled expression. Richard just whispered, "She's just being silly. Don't let it bother you." Dixie smiled, though she still didn't know what to say. Her dress only had a tad bit of white lace on her collar. What *could* she say?

Cousin Jennifer Rains came to the rescue with "Now Constance Angelica, a little white makes an outfit cheery! It looks nice on you, Dixianna. I've missed you so much."

Dixie gave Jenny a hug. "I've missed you too. It's been so long! At least a year and a half!" she exclaimed. Constance Angelica seemed upset that Dixie hadn't become angry with her. She flounced away to the other end of the room.

Every one exchanged greetings, then broke off into groups to talk. Silas was talking with the uncles and Papa Rains, while the ladies went to the sewing room to help Nana with a quilt she was working on and to talk. Richard, Charles Tinderman II, Allen and Drew Cameron, and Philip were included in the elder men's conversation, and the rest of the boys bundled up to play in the snow. Seth was invited to join the men's talk, but the younger boys pleaded for him to play with them, and they won out. The other boys promised to join them later.

The girls decided to go upstairs to Jennifer's room so they could talk and knit, away from the menfolk's conversation.

★ 1861 ★

Later that evening, Ellen was looking over an old childhood sketchbook of Carol Tinderman's. Her older sister seemed distracted. "Carol, is something wrong?"

Carol stopped pacing and sat down near Ellen. "I don't know how to put it into words, Ellen. It's just…well the boys…" she stopped and tried again. "We all know war is coming. No one wants to admit it, but we all know it. The boys want to join the army when it happens. Christopher is still too young, but that's not what bothers me the most. Ellen, neither of the boys have ever placed their trust in Christ. How can I let them go to war knowing if they die…?"

"Oh, Carol, I didn't realize. Well, I had wondered about Christopher, because of some things he had written to Seth, but I wasn't sure," Ellen said.

Carol nodded. "Their salvation means everything to me. Christina is the only one who has professed faith in Christ. But not the boys or Constance Angelica. This worries me day and night. Ellen, please help me pray about this!"

Ellen reached out and grasped her sister's hand. "Of course I will. Let's pray right now." The two bowed their heads, and Ellen began to pray.

"Dear Lord, we come to You with a heavy burden for Carol's unsaved children. We are concerned for their souls and where they will spend eternity. Lord, please soften their hearts toward You. Please let us be good examples and witnesses for You. Please let us see them come to You before it's too late. In Jesus' name I pray, Amen."

The sisters hugged and Carol dried her eyes. "Thank you, Ellen. Thank you."

★ 1861 ★

They had their family picture taken on Thursday. Silas and Ellen decided it was time to talk with Ellen's parents about their beliefs. They asked to talk with them in Mr. Rains' study. When everyone was situated, Mr. Rains said, "You both look troubled. What is wrong?"

Ellen spoke first. "Father, we know how you feel about the present developments between the North and South." She looked at her husband.

Silas spoke up, "We simply wish to agree to disagree on this subject. Maybe the states are stronger united, but we feel the Lord leading us to support the Southern cause."

He finished, waiting for Mr. Rains to respond. The silence hung in the air like a dark cloud. Mr. Rains seemed angry. "You mean to tell me that you plan to lead part of this family into this rebellion? Don't think that this only affects you, Silas. You married my daughter, and this affects all of us!"

Silas remained calm. "Sir, I understand that. I know this affects the whole family. But your decision affects us as well. We have prayed about what we should do ever since the first secession. And we…"

"Prayed? And you think we haven't?" Mr. Rains interrupted as he stood to his feet.

"I know this isn't easy for either of us. Y'all are our family, and we love you. But we want to disagree peaceably. We want no hard feelings to come between us. Please try to understand our position."

Ellen glanced across the room at her mother who was already wiping tears from her eyes. Ellen had bravely fought back her own tears up to this point.

"The way I see it, the only peaceable thing to do is to stay in the Union," countered Mr. Rains. "Stay where it's safe. Silas, you're a sensible man. Stop and think about what you are doing."

"I understand, sir, what you're saying. But I have to do what I believe is best for my family."

Mr. Rains turned away to collect his thoughts. At last he turned toward them. "Silas, to be completely honest, I believe you are wrong. But I can't make these decisions for you, I know that. What does it matter anyway? You agree with the South, I agree with the North. You are right, there's no reason to split the family over it."

He hugged his daughter and son-in-law. Mrs. Rains did likewise. They talked for another hour before praying together and parting.

Papa Rains announced the Mason's decision at the evening meal. Philip looked sorrowfully at Richard. Richard knew what he was thinking: They might be fighting against each other someday.

Christopher fidgeted in the seat next to Seth. Wallace Culwright nearly strangled on his water and had to leave the room with a coughing fit. Upon his return, he whispered to Drew, "I wasn't expecting to hear that!"

"Me neither. Since Uncle Silas used to be in the Army, I figured he'd be for us."

Allison whispered to Dixie, "We can't let this come between us. We have to stick together as a family, differences and all." Dixie nodded and gave a sigh of relief.

One of the younger cousins mouthed "Rebel," across the table at Michael, who chose to ignore it.

For the most part, the family seemed to take the news fairly well. But of course, Constance Angelica was not going to keep her feelings a secret. After the meal, she told Dixie that she and her family were traitors. Constance failed to keep her conversation in a low tone. In fact, she practically yelled at Dixie. As a result, she was sent to her room by her father for the evening.

In spite of Constance Angelica, the Masons enjoyed the remainder of their trip and regretted they could only stay a week. But Saturday came, and the Masons returned to their home in Four Tree Springs, North Carolina.

★ 1861 ★

February and March seemed to fly by. Mr. and Mrs. Mason were making plans for a trip to England to renew their cotton contract. Silas' nephew, Isaac Mason and his wife Lydia where coming to stay with the children while they were gone. They would be leaving for England on April 2nd.

The reality of war crept closer and closer. Dixie and Michael kept close tabs on the newspaper headlines, and Seth filled in the gaps with news from work.

They found out that on March 1st, the U.S. Congress refused to consider Virginia's peace conference proposals. This greatly offended the people of Virginia, and there was now talk that they might secede.

There was also fear in the north for the U.S. troops stationed at Fort Sumter[4]. The officer in charge, Major Robert Anderson[5] had reported a food shortage and said that they might have to evacuate.

On the 6th of March, the Confederacy called for 100,000 volunteers and on the 11th, the Confederate constitution was adopted permanently. Michael's mind raced with excitement. Would North Carolina one day become a part of the new country? He personally hoped so.

★1861★

---

[4] Ft. Sumter is located off shore of Charleston, S.C.
[5] Union Major Robert Anderson commanded Ft. Sumter until its surrender in April. He went on to serve the U.S. Military during the war.

Chapter 4

★

God Has a Plan

Lead me, O Lord, in thy righteousness because of mine enemies;
make thy way straight before my face.
Psalm 5:8

Bang! went the screen door. "Mama! Mama, where are you?" Michael hurried toward the kitchen as Dixie entered behind him, though much more quietly, carrying a stack of papers to grade.

"I'm in the back parlor. Michael, please don't be so loud in the house. It isn't polite."

"Yes Ma'am. I'm sorry."

Dixie took a seat next to Mama. "Michael, did you tell Mama about the Tanners?" Michael shook his head.

"What about them, children? This better not be gossip," Mama warned.

"Oh, no, Mama! It ain't gossip," Michael said quickly. "Mr. Tanner and Brandon came to the general store after school let out. They were buying a whole bunch of stuff. Mr. Tanner was upset because something was out of stock. He said, 'This is one reason we are moving back to Delaware. They always have what you need, when you need it.' Then Brandon told us that

40

they're moving next week. Richard tried to steer the conversation toward spiritual things, but Mr. Tanner interrupted saying they had to go."

Mama shook her head. "I was afraid of this. Mrs. Tanner asked me to pray against a possible move."

Just then, they heard a horse cantering toward the house. Dixie looked out the window. "Oh! Seth must've gotten off early. Here he comes. But he sure doesn't look happy." Michael hurried to put Charger in the barn, which was one of his favorite tasks.

Seth came in wearing a downcast expression. "Seth, what's wrong son?" Mama asked.

Seth looked up and said, "Mr. Burton's reducing his staff. He went around to all his workers and asked which side we would fight for if war broke out. I don't know what the others said, but me and Tyler Nace said Confederacy. And the next thing we know, we were told we were no longer needed."

"Oh, Seth, that's terrible! I had no idea Mr. Burton sided with the north!" Mama exclaimed. "I'm sure his daughter and son-in-law are shocked! They are pro-Confederacy," she said, referring to their neighbors, the Shaynes.

Seth continued. "I didn't know he was a Yankee either. Everyone working for him is between fifteen and eighteen years old. I reckon it's not as bad as firing a man with a family to feed."

Mama looked sympathetically at her son. "Well, you were about to cut back to part time anyway, with cotton time coming and all. And if Tyler needs a job, I'm sure your father would appreciate another hand in the fields."

"I guess so. It's just embarrassing getting fired! I just wish he hadn't done it. And I was hoping to enroll in medical school this fall. How am I gonna get in now?" Seth sighed. "I don't have a job to help with my tuition! Maybe God has something else in mind, although I'm sure I don't know what it is. Oh, I almost forgot."

He dug into his pocket and withdrew an envelope. "Richard asked me to give this to you and Papa. It's from Sheriff

Gallimore, and Richard said he wanted y'all's input before he made his decision."

Mama nodded and placed the envelope in her skirt pocket. Dixie moved to a nearby table to begin grading papers. Michael ran upstairs, presumably to do his homework. Seth went up as well but returned a few minutes later in his work clothes. He quickly headed for the barn to muck out the stalls.

Dixie sat deep in thought. Mama turned and looked at her daughter. "Dixie, you look awful somber. What's bothering you?"

"Oh, Mama, it ain't right! Mr. Burton knew Seth was saving up to go to medical school. Our county needs another good doctor. He's been doing advanced studies at night to get the education he'd need to be accepted at the school. Why did this have to happen? He would have been ready to go by this fall."

Mama put her arm around Dixie. "I'm sure Seth is wondering the same thing. But God has a plan. He sees the whole picture even when we can't. Besides, with war looming, I doubt Seth would be able to get in the school. Did you know that the North still thinks they'll be able to bring us back into the Union without a war? They think if they keep pressing the issue enough that we'll 'come to our senses,' and the 'rebellion' will be over!"

Dixie laughed. "That's silly! They need to wake up and see what's going on right in front of them! Of course, we don't want to fight them, but if they threaten us, we have the right to defend ourselves!"

Mama laughed and nodded in agreement. "Anything else on your mind?"

Dixie shrugged. "Oh, just thinking about y'all's trip to England. How long are y'all gonna be gone?"

"About a month. You know it takes a long time to renew a cotton contract."

Dixie nodded. She dreaded cotton time. They had a hand powered cotton gin, and everyone had to take their turn turning the crank. It felt as though it was only yesterday that they had been seeding cotton. Next week they would be planting cotton again. Harvest time was in September. During that time, Dixie truly felt that she was "in a land of cotton," as the song, *Dixieland* goes.

★ 1861 ★

That night, after everyone was in bed, Silas and Ellen read the sheriff's note. It read:

Mr. Richard Mason,

I leave for South Carolina on the 9th. I have business to conduct with some friends of mine. I wish to tell you of my plans once I get to S.C. I have secessionist friends in Charleston, and we agreed that action must be taken to regain Fort Sumter. This ought to give us a stronger foothold in our land. I would like for you to accompany me on this errand. Duty beckons us to take action for the generations to come. I need to know your answer soon.

Kevin N. Gallimore.

"I don't like it," Silas declared. "They're just asking for war. Let the Yank's take their time. They keep putting it off, so let's have peace while we can."

Ellen nodded. "I don't want my boy going off and starting fights."

"I agree, although God has given me peace about him going to war if there is one. He's a strong Christian, he's trustworthy, and I believe that may be what God wants for him. I know he and Seth have been praying about it. But defending your country and picking fights are two different things."

After a time of prayer, they met with Richard and shared their feelings with him. "But," Silas reminded, "You're a man

43

now and have to make this decision on your own. We can't make it for you."

Richard sighed with relief. "Those are my feelings too, Papa. I just wanted to see how y'all felt. I'm not going."

★ 1861 ★

The next couple of days were a blur of activity. Richard gave Sheriff Gallimore his answer. He was a bit disappointed, but he understood Richard's view of things.

The children pitched in to help with the packing for their parents' trip. Their cousin Isaac and his wife, Lydia, came to watch over things while the parents were gone. Lydia was expecting their first baby.

The next day, Silas and Ellen boarded the train that would take them to the coast. From there they would take a ship to England. Farewells were shouted to the travelers as the train pulled out.

After the train was out of sight, Dixie and Michael walked to school. It was hard for Dixie to get her mind on teaching; goodbyes were not easy for her.

Richard headed for work, and the others started for home. Isaac and Seth were going to meet with the tenant workers to start plowing the cotton fields, including the fields that were lying dormant.

On the way to the house, Tyler joined them, since he was going to be helping out with the plowing. His duties on his family's indigo farm were taken care of, and he was glad for the extra work.

A friendship between him and Seth had come about during the last couple of months. Mr. and Mrs. Nace were thrilled that Tyler was starting to open up more. And yet there was still something there…something they couldn't put their finger on. It was almost as if Tyler were in inward tumult.

Seth sensed this too, but didn't bring attention to it. If Tyler wanted to talk about it, he would bring it up.

Tyler was indeed in tumult. Before, Tyler had been an outgoing young man who never knew a stranger. Their family held a fair social standing in Baltimore, and he had enjoyed the privileges that came with this prominence.

Then one day all that changed. There had been a gathering at the home of an upper-class church member. The guests of honor were a Pastor's family from out west. They had been evangelizing the Indians in their area, accomplishing much for the cause of Christ.

Their son James was around Tyler's age and engaged the young men in stories of the Indians and their mission work among them. Tyler was captivated by the sacrifices the family had made to reach the natives.

Then James said, "I can't believe some Christians do not see that we are all called to be missionaries, at home or abroad. Every Christian should have the desire to serve God in any capacity; whether in fulltime service or not, we are called to serve God, not ourselves!"

That had set Tyler to thinking. He had never felt inclined to share his faith with anyone. He'd never thought of doing a thing to further the cause of Christ beyond tithing, and even that was more out of duty than anything else.

As Tyler pondered these things, he couldn't shake certain feelings. And these new feelings really troubled him. He slept fitfully at night. He no longer took pleasure in his old pastimes or acquaintances. It all seemed so frivolous to him now.

If only Tyler had known that it was the prick of the Holy Spirit, seeking to drawn him to a higher call of duty to his Savior. But instead, Tyler struggled on.

Soon everyone reached the first field. After delegating who would plow what part of the field and which sections still needed "de-rocking", they began the work.

The next few days brought rumors of fighting in the future. On April 4th, the Union's President, Abraham Lincoln[6] ordered a relief expedition to Fort Sumter. On the 8th of April, the expedition set sail from New York to help the bottled up Union soldiers.

Michael couldn't help but wonder what the result of the expedition would be. Somehow, he felt that no matter what happened, it wouldn't be without a good deal of action.

★ 1861 ★

---

[6] The 16th President of the United States. Lincoln passionately agreed with and led the Union in a war against the new Confederate nation.

Chapter 5

★

Lighting the Fire

The next morning went smoothly. Michael headed for the
train station before school with Dixie following close
behind. They shouted "Fare-well," to the Tanners as they
boarded the north bound train. Dixie handed Matilda a flower.
Matilda had tears in her eyes as she hugged her friend. "I'll
write; I promise. Papa said I could. I won't forget you."

After saying farewell to people two days in a row, it
seemed to Michael that everyone was leaving! But he was
relieved that at least his parents were returning in a few weeks!

Everyone in the one room schoolhouse was downhearted.
The girls missed Matilda. The fourteen year old had always been
a ray of sunshine, quite the contrast to her twenty year old bully
of a brother. Michael couldn't count the times Brandon had

come to the store with the express purpose of causing trouble for Richard.

Time passed as it always does. Richard worked at the store, Isaac and Seth plowed the fields, Lydia and Dixie helped Mrs. Bradley with the house and Michael went to school. With everything going the way it usually did, no one could have known that the very next week would be the beginning of the biggest conflict they had ever experienced, a conflict that would change their lives forever.

★ 1861 ★

Dixie walked through town toward home after picking up the mail. Dixie, deep in thought over an English lesson she was to teach soon, didn't pay much attention to those around her.

"Hey, you! Get out of the way!"

Dixie jerked her head up just in time to see Martha Alistair, a classmate of Michael's, step timidly out of the way of three mounted soldiers. Dixie studied their uniforms. Privates. Her cousin Philip had taught her how to tell what rank a soldier was by looking at the patches on the uniforms they wore.

"Badin, that's no way to talk to a lady." The soldier dismounted and walked toward Martha, who backed away from him. "Are you alright?" Martha just nodded.

Badin huffed impatiently. "Come on, Evans! What is my father going to say if we are late getting back? Now come on!" Evans sighed and mounted his horse. He waved to Martha and rode off with the others. They passed Dixie on the way, and the one called Badin glared down at her as he passed. Dixie pretended not to notice.

Martha dashed past Dixie and entered her father's bank. Just then, Howard Wheeling, one of the newsboys, rushed toward Dixie. Out of breath, he handed Dixie a telegram. "Oh, thanks. You run telegrams now?"

"Yeah, Mr. Burton's too busy to do it today. Sure miss Seth at the office."

"He misses it too."

"See y'all at church!" Howard called as he hurried away.

The telegram was from Pastor Brewster, who was visiting family in South Carolina. They lived not far from Fort Sumter in Charleston. It was addressed to her father, so she took it to Richard at the general store.

"Richard! Richard, where are you?" she called searching the empty store. Both he and Mr. Spencer came out of the back room. She handed him the telegram, which he opened and read it to himself.

Confederates fired on Fort Sumter. Still at it.
Pastor B.

"Oh no," was all he could say. He handed Mr. Spencer the note. Concern was apparent on his face. Dixie looked at her older brother searchingly. At last she was handed the telegram.

Mr. Spencer shook his head. "Lord, please help us."

★1861★

Tears slid down cousin Lydia's cheeks when the rest of the family heard the news. Isaac pulled her close to him and said, "Dear, the Yankees have been asking for this for a long time. They've pushed us too far. Maybe it won't go any farther than this incident. The North needs to know that we are sick of tyranny. We have rights too! But, it's tragic none the less. Let's pray that no souls are lost in the conflict."

Mr. Bradley slowly walked out of the room without comment. He was a quiet man who usually kept his opinions to himself. The Mason children knew the older man well enough to know he was probably going to a quiet place to pray.

Dixie's heart stopped racing, and an overwhelming sense of security in Christ swept over her. She stepped outside on the porch to be alone and to collect her thoughts. Suddenly she had a strange feeling that she wasn't alone. She glanced around but saw no one. She couldn't shake the feeling, however, and decided to go back inside.

As she opened the door, she was certain she heard a noise. *Probably just an animal,* she thought, putting the whole thing out of her mind as she went to see if Mrs. Bradley needed any help in the kitchen.

★1861★

Dixie spent the next morning cleaning the house with Mrs. Bradley until dinner time. After the meal, Dixie worked on a sewing project while Lydia rested in the back parlor.

Meanwhile at the store, Richard was waiting on Mrs. Armistead, a very trying task. She supposed she needed a pound of cornmeal, but she'd better get two just in case there was a sudden shortage. She needed yarn. Blue would be best, no, green or maybe gray, but the purple was overly tempting. Yellow should do the trick, but black was more practical. Richard sighed in near exasperation as she instructed him to get down two skeins of pale pink yarn.

She's the most indecisive woman I've ever seen! Mr. Armistead must be a very patient man. Richard thought as Mrs. Armistead scanned her list.

"Let me see…Oh, yes. I need some tack nails." Richard quickly found the desired item and set it on the counter.

"Will that be all, Mrs. Armistead?"

"Yes, I believe so. I want a receipt so I know you're not cheating me." Richard laughed inwardly as he wrote up the bill.

"Your total comes to $2.28."

"Dear me, prices do increase, don't they?"

"Sure do, ma'am."

"Well, here you go," she said, handing him $2.10. Not noticing her mistake, she left. Richard sighed and started to write a bill out for the missing $.18. He stopped, and withdrew two dimes from his pocket. He dropped them into the cash register and took two pennies as change. *There, now she won't have to worry about it.*

Richard waited for the next customer. The next person who entered the store was Howard Wheeling. "Telegram for y'all. It's from South Carolina." Richard took the telegram and looked at his pocket watch. It was closing time. Mr. Spencer dismissed him, and Richard headed home.

When he reached home, Dixie was on the front porch knitting. Michael hurried out the door toward the barn to help Seth and Isaac with the evening chores but stopped when he saw Richard with the telegram. He walked back up the porch steps as his brother read aloud.

Fort Sumter surrendered. We won! Be home on the 16th. Pastor B.

Michael threw his hat into the air, revealing his messy brown hair. "Yahoo! Hurrah for the Confederates!" Dixie smiled at his excitement. The noise brought Seth and Isaac running out of the barn.

"What happened?" Seth panted.

Dixie explained, "Fort Sumter surrendered! The South won! So Michael's celebrating." Everyone was thrilled with the news.

"I hope that'll settle things. This should prove to wake the Yanks up," Isaac said encouragingly.

Lydia joined the group and excited conversation continued. But Dixie couldn't help feeling someone was watching her again.

She jerked her head up and thought she saw a dark figure slip behind a tree. *It's just my imagination. Or maybe a stray dog's back there,* she thought as the group headed inside for apple pie and sweet tea.

"Have you boys gotten into the pies already?" asked Mrs. Bradley.

The boys looked at each other. "No. We know better than to go near them without permission," Richard replied.

Mrs. Bradley furrowed her brow. "I set two outside to cool earlier and now one is missing."

"You probably just forgot you only made one this time," Mr. Bradley teased.

"Dixie, did I not set two pies out there to cool?" Mrs. Bradley asked.

"Yes, you did," Dixie replied, "Because I offered to carry one and you said you could handle it."

Michael sat up straight on the bench. "There's a pie thief on the loose! Get the Sheriff!"

Richard laughed. "One pie ain't worth calling him over; besides, he's in South Carolina. So instead of bellyaching over that one, let's make *this* one disappear too!"

★ 1861 ★

On Monday morning, Dixie and Michael headed for school. As they walked into the schoolhouse they sensed something was wrong. Mr. Pierce's usual cheery face was downcast.

He stood in front of the class, cleared his throat and said, "I'm closing school early this year. After today there will be no more classes for this school term. And I probably won't be returning next school year." The students looked at each other in bewilderment. He was closing school a month early? And not coming back? It couldn't be! What would the students do without their beloved teacher? Even Dixie didn't know what he was talking about.

"I've enlisted in the county militia. In the event of war, we will take up arms against the northern army. I believe it is my duty to fight for my rights and my students' rights. This is a cause worth fighting for. I have peace with God to defend the South."

Some students began to cry. Mr. Pierce continued, "I've recruited Miss Brewster to teach you this coming school year. Please respect her and please be understanding in my decision."

Dixie held onto her much used handkerchief. Mr. Pierce dismissed them at 8:30 after giving them their end of the year grades. He hugged each of his students before they left.

Dixie was the last one to leave. As she walked out the door, Mr. Pierce handed her a book entitled, *Illnesses and*

Treatments by Dr. Arnold Pierce. Dixie looked up at her former teacher for an explanation.

"My father wrote it. You and Seth both show a strong interest in this area and I thought y'all might find this book interesting. I hope it will be a help to you and your family."

The tears flooded back into Dixie's eyes. "Thank you, Mr. Pierce."

★1861★

Later that day, Seth took Dixie to the horse sale. It was held just outside of town, and it was huge! Men, women and children darted here and there. Seth and Dixie made their way through the crowd in search of the perfect horses.

Richard was there as well, looking for some bargains on horse tack for Mr. Spencer, his boss at the general store. Seth and Dixie were glad for his presence, as he was going to help them pick a good horse.

They saw many different breeds, from Appaloosas to Quarter horses as well as Palominos and Thoroughbreds. Dixie thought a great deal of them were pretty, but she was more interested in personality. "Can we look at some Mustangs?"

"Sure, why not," Richard replied. They found them easily enough, but none were really what Dixie was looking for.

She turned to go to another corral but stopped when something caught her eye. "Oh! He's beautiful!"

Seth's eyes widened and Richard nodded in agreement as he said, "Let's go look at him."

Chapter 6

★

Confederate and Lady

A righteous man regardeth the life of his beast: but the tender
mercies of the wicked are cruel.
Proverbs 12:10

◇◇★◇◇

"A horse is a thing of beauty...none will tire of looking at him as
long as he displays himself in his splendor."
Xenophon

The mustang stallion was beautiful, but he seemed very timid. He was dark gray with a jet black mane and tail. A black dorsal stripe stretched majestically from his mane to his tail.

Dixie was mesmerized. As they watched, the horse began to prance. Two soldiers approached the horse. It pranced to the other side of the corral. One threw a rope around the stallion's neck. The horse shied away from the soldier but didn't put up much of a fuss.

The soldiers proceeded to saddle and bridle the mustang. The horse fought the bit a little, but after some coaxing from one of the soldiers, he finally took it into his mouth.

A man in an officer's uniform stepped up and mounted the horse. Dixie winced when she saw a riding whip in the man's hand. Richard watched horse and rider carefully. The horse acted so nervous.

"Hup, Boston. Get up, Boston, move!" The horse refused to budge, so the man applied his spurs. Still the horse wouldn't move. Angry, the officer used the whip. The horse bucked and the rider went tumbling to the ground.

One of the soldiers regained control of the horse. "I'll teach you not to buck me off, you crazy beast!" He came towards the horse, whip in hand. Dixie turned away as she heard the whip make contact with the poor animal's hide.

"Have you decided not to keep him after all?" one of the soldiers asked when at last the whipping stopped.

"Yes! Sell him to the first person who will take him! I despise timid animals as well as one who bucks! If he won't sell, put it down."

Dixie looked over at her brothers. Richard whispered, "Pet him and see how he acts." The siblings walked up to the soldier who was treating the whip marks on the horse's flank.

"May we take a look at your horse?" Richard asked.

The soldier looked up. "He belongs to Capt. Badin, but you are welcome to look him over."

Dixie reached out a hand towards the horse's nose. He sidled away at first, but eventually, he sniffed her hand and allowed her to stroke his neck. His muscles quivered under her touch but ever so slightly began to relax. "You're a beautiful horse; you know that?" she asked softly.

The soldier grinned. "He's great when there are no whips around. He's just jumpy." He watched as Dixie admired the horse and as her brothers looked over his general fitness. Richard pointed out some qualities to Seth that were important to look for in a good horse.

Richard was impressed. "He's a sound animal. How much is he going for?"

"Well, by himself, Capt. Badin wants $100. But he's also selling the stallion's match. She is a pretty little thing, and well built. She's expecting her first colt. If you want them, I can let you have them for $200.00."

Dixie looked at her brothers eagerly. Horses usually cost at least $150 apiece. This was a great savings. Seth seemed interested. "May I see the mare?" he asked.

"Follow me." The man led them to another corral. The mare *was* beautiful. She was a buckskin with the same beautiful black mane, tail, and dorsal stripe as the stallion. She was strong in build and looked as though she would make a good cavalry horse. Seth liked her and she had Richard's stamp of approval right off.

"Do they answer to specific names?" asked Dixie.

"Not the stallion. Capt. Badin calls him Boston. The girl's Rebel Lady and she answers to it. They are both three years old. Do you want them?"

"May we discuss this for a moment?" Richard asked. The soldier nodded, and the trio walked a few feet away to talk. "I like the mare, and the stallion is in great condition, but he seems a bit on the timid side," Richard whispered.

"Better to be timid than wild," Dixie reasoned. "I think that man's beaten it into him. The soldier said he was fine without whips."

Richard nodded in agreement. "Oh, he looks like a fine horse. I just know it'll take some work to get his trust. But if you're up to it, I'd go ahead."

"I'd like to try."

"Let's pray about it." As Richard prayed, Dixie could feel the Yankees staring at them. When they finished, they agreed that they should buy the pair. "Sir, you've got yourself a deal," Richard said.

The soldier nodded with satisfaction. "Good. Pvt. Badin, get the horses for them."

As Richard handed the soldier the money, Dixie recognized the soldier who was bringing the horses. It was the soldier that had yelled at Martha only days before. He was back!

She glanced back at the soldier who they had been talking to. Of course! It was Pvt. Evans, the kind Yankee, as Dixie had labeled him.

Pvt. Badin looked at Dixie as though he was trying to figure out where he had seen her before. Dixie turned away, his stare making her nervous. As he handed the lead rope to Richard, his eyes narrowed at Dixie.

Dixie couldn't think of any reason he should be mad at her. After all, she hadn't done anything wrong. He was the one that had done wrong by yelling at Martha, not her. She ignored his scowl and followed her brothers toward the main road.

Richard told them he was excited to find several saddles and bridles in fair condition at a good price. Mr. Spencer was stock piling just in case there was a sudden rush for horse tack. They knew he meant if war broke out; he would be sold out to Cavalry men in a flash.

When they reached home, Isaac and Michael were out in the back field. Richard hitched Champion up to a small cart and went back to town to pick up the supplies he'd purchased for the store. Seth headed out to the field after he helped Dixie stable the horses.

Dixie lingered in the barn, stroking her horse's neck. She could feel tenseness as she did this, but as before, he began to relax. "You know boy, Boston don't fit you. You need a good Southern name...like Confederate. I can't think of a better name for you."

The stallion stretched his neck out over the stall door and placed his head on Dixie's shoulder. Dixie stroked his glossy mane. After a few moments, he turned to look at the feed Seth had poured in the feed box.

Dixie headed for the house to see if Mrs. Bradley needed help with anything. Then she remembered the blackberry jam pie she'd made earlier. It was surely cooled by now.

She walked around to the back of the house to retrieve her pie. She stopped suddenly and slowly backed away. There on the back steps stood a black bear! Eating her pie!

Panic welled up inside her. It wasn't full grown, probably a year or two old. The bear climbed down from the porch and meandered toward the fields. *Oh no!* she thought. *The boys!*

★1861★

"Get up Dolly! Come on Mort. Get up there!" Isaac shouted at his mule team. Mort was pulling as hard as he could, but Dolly had planted her rear legs in the dirt and laid her ears back. She wasn't about to move.

Isaac closed his eyes and placed his hand on his forehead in exasperation. This was the sixth time in a row that Dolly had refused to move. Tyler and Seth had tried everything they could think of; coaxing, shouting, anything to get her going.

Michael had even tried to help them by prodding her along with sticks, but nothing worked. Michael had given up and gone to get a drink of water from the bucket in the nearby wagon.

"I don't know what to tell you, Isaac. Have they ever given you trouble before?" Seth asked, wiping sweat off his forehead.

Isaac shrugged. "I haven't used them before. I bought them right before we came here."

Just then, Richard rode up on Champion, finally home from work. He had seen the whole thing as he came across the field. He grinned to himself as he looked at his "city boy" cousin's attempt to work the team.

Isaac's father was a businessman. Isaac had been born and raised in Raleigh, North Carolina's capital city. It wasn't until two years ago that Isaac had done any farm work, but this was his first year working with stubborn mules.

Richard dismounted, winked at Michael, and walked over to Isaac. Placing his hand on Isaac's shoulder, he said, "Isaac, hang onto the plow and I'll get the mules moving."

Isaac shrugged and took hold of the plow handles. Before Isaac knew what was happening, Richard had whipped off his hat and popped Dolly with it. Although it didn't hurt her, the sudden movement and sting the hat produced scared Dolly. She took off across the field with Mort and Isaac in tow. The whole thing happened in less time than it takes to describe it.

By the time they reached the other end of the field, Dolly had slowed to a canter. Isaac turned the team around and directed them toward the others. He stopped the team and walked toward Richard with one of those "I'm gonna get you," looks.

Richard threw his hands up in front of himself, and started backing up in mock fear. "Hey, um, uh Isaac, I *did* get the team to start. Um, hmm, no hard feelings, right?" Isaac kept walking toward him.

Michael jumped into the back of the wagon to watch out of the way. Seth and Tyler leaned up against the side of the wagon to enjoy the show. Richard smiled nervously, then bolted across the field with Isaac at his heels. It would be fun to see if Isaac would catch the fastest runner in Four Tree Springs.

By now, the tenant workers had all heard the laughter and stopped to watch the chase, cheering the boys on.

Richard raced back toward the wagon, darting around the mules as he ran. Isaac ran around the other side of the wagon and collided with Richard, sending both young men to the ground. Richard scrambled to his feet, but Isaac had a hold on the bottom of Richard's shirt. He then pinned Richard down by the shoulders.

"Give up?" Isaac asked with a smirk of satisfaction. Sweat was streaming down both of their faces. Richard panted for breath, laughing in between gasps as he nodded that he was done running.

Isaac helped him up and the two laughed at each other's appearance. Richard's reddish brown hair was now completely brown. The dirt was more noticeable in Isaac's white blonde hair. The boys quickly dusted themselves off and shook the dirt out of their hair.

The younger boys were laughing in the safety of the wagon. Dolly and Mort seemed to be laughing with their donkey like brays. Champion whinnied his approval too.

Seth said, "If y'all are done with your childishness, its supper time. Let's go!"

Suddenly, the boys heard a noise; a snarly, roaring noise. They turned and saw the bear stretched out under a tree at the edge of the field. Michael's eyes widened. Champion and the mules began to fidget.

"What do we do?" Seth whispered to Richard. One look at Isaac's face told them he wasn't sure.

"We'll have to shoot it. If we start for home, it may follow us and if we stay here, he may charge us. He seems antsy. Tyler, pass me the rifle."

Tyler passed the gun to Richard. He quickly loaded it and raised the rifle to his shoulder as the bear stood and began to come towards them.

Just as Richard fired the gun, the bear dropped to all fours, causing the bullet to whiz right over its head. The sound startled the bear, which whirled around and took off for nearby Mt. Dogwood.

"The Cherokee up there will get him if he causes trouble," Richard remarked. It was too late for another shot. The boys gathered their things and headed for the house to make sure the bear hadn't already been there.

★ 1861 ★

Michael burst through the kitchen door, and he and Dixie began talking at the same time about the bear. The other guys walked in as Dixie and Mrs. Bradley were putting food on the table, still talking about the bear.

"And so, Michael, we found the pie thief. And now I know what I saw in the back yard a couple of days ago. It wasn't a dog. It was that bear!" Dixie concluded. After the fact, they could laugh about the encounters, though Michael lamented the loss of the blackberry pie.

A few days later, they heard from a neighbor that the Indians had indeed taken care of the bear. That was a relief to the townspeople. They all knew how destructive bears could be.

★ 1861 ★

60

April sped by rapidly. The Brewsters returned on the 16th as promised, but Lana declared she wouldn't tell the details of what she'd seen concerning Fort Sumter until she could get the Naces and Masons together at her house. Dixie groaned inside. That could take weeks!

Seth and Dixie worked hard gentling their horses. Lady wasn't a problem; she loved Seth and it showed. But Confederate took some time. He needed lots of love and attention to get his trust.

Richard helped Dixie get Confederate used to people riding him without bucking them off. He had bucked Richard a couple times, but when he realized there wasn't a whip, he had calmed right down. Now, Dixie could ride him without a hitch.

In the political realm, things were busy. On the 15th of April, U.S. President Lincoln called for 75,000 volunteers for the Union military. Then Virginia seceded on the 17th.

A man from Virginia, Col. Robert E. Lee[7], was offered the command of the Union forces, which he declined, and on the 20th of April, he resigned his commission in the army. This name was not unknown in the Mason household, for Papa had often told of the brave officer he'd met during the Mexican War. Michael was glad to find out about the colonel's resignation from the Army.

---

[7] Former officer in the United States Army. He resigned his office on April 20th, 1861 and later became the Commander of the Army of Northern Virginia.

Chapter 7

★

Something Worth Fighting For

*Now the Lord is that Spirit: and where the Spirit of the Lord is,
there is liberty.*
II Corinthians 3:17

April 20th was just another day for the Masons. With morning chores done, Dixie met Annie Nace and Lana to take a walk through town. It was nice getting to spend time with each other. Schedules had prevented that lately.

Many people were out and about on this warm day. People went from store to store buying things and chatting with each other.

Before dinnertime the girls headed to Dixie's house to do some needle work. Lydia would be helping Mrs. Bradley and had told Dixie earlier to enjoy her time with her friends.

They hurried up the path to the house and entered the kitchen. Lydia was nowhere in sight and Mrs. Bradley said she hadn't come down yet and was too busy getting food for the workers to stop and look for her. "That's strange. She's usually down way before now. Lydia! Lydia, where are you?" Dixie called as she ran up the stairs.

"Dixie? Oh, good you're home. Could you come in here?" Lydia called from the guest room.

"Sure." Dixie hurried down the hall. There was something strange about Lydia's voice and that quickened Dixie's pace even more.

Dixie opened the door to Lydia's room and found her lying in bed in her night gown. "What's the matter? Are you alright?" Dixie asked in alarm.

Lydia's face was pale. She looked at Dixie. "The baby's coming. I need the midwife. I ..."

"Don't worry, Lydia. We'll get the midwife. Lana's here too, and she's helped Miss Faber deliver babies before," Dixie said briskly. Lydia closed her eyes and nodded.

Dixie practically flew down the stairs. "Annie! Do you know where Miss Faber lives?"

"Yes."

"Good. You run get her here as soon as possible. The baby's coming! Lana, I think she needs you. What should I do?"

Annie raced out the door as Lana jumped into action. "Dixie, get some clean linens and ask Mrs. Bradley to put some water on to boil. Miss Faber will need it later."

"Should I get Isaac?" Dixie asked.

Lana shook her head. "No! He'd just be in the way."

Dixie hurried off to carry out the tasks while Lana went upstairs with Lydia. When the water was ready, Dixie and Mrs. Bradley brought the things upstairs.

Midwife Faber entered the room moments later. When her job was done, Dixie went downstairs with Annie and Mrs. Bradley. Lana stood next to Lydia and held her hand. She began to pray as the delivery began.

Before long, Lydia was holding her newborn baby. Tears fell softly from her eyes onto the small child. Lana's eyes were moist as well. Lydia relaxed, holding the infant tenderly in her arms.

 ★ 1861 ★

Downstairs, Annie and Dixie sat at the table eating. "I hope everything goes alright," Annie said nervously. "I hope the baby's healthy." Dixie grinned at her worried friend. Just then, they heard the baby's cry. "It's here!" Annie shouted, and then gave a sigh of relief.

Dixie said, "Thank the Lord. Let's get a tray of food ready to take up soon. I know she's gonna be hungry. Mrs. Bradley hasn't come back in from feeding the workers yet."

Moments later, Isaac and the others entered the kitchen from the field. Both girls began talking to them at once, but were interrupted by another cry from the baby. Isaac, Seth, Tyler and Michael looked toward the staircase in surprise.

Suddenly, reality hit Isaac. "The baby! Lydia's had the baby!" Dixie nodded as Isaac headed for the stairs. The girls stayed behind to serve the boys the noon meal.

Isaac met Miss Faber in the hallway. "Ah! Isaac, you're already here," the midwife said, smiling. "I was afraid I was gonna have to send the girls after you. Come in." Isaac hesitated, and then entered the room.

Lydia smiled at him. "It's a girl, Isaac. We have a precious baby girl." Isaac sat on the bed next to his wife and daughter. Isaac hugged Lydia gently.

"She's beautiful, just like her mama," he replied.

A few minutes later, Miss Faber and Lana came down for a bite to eat. Dixie jumped up to fix their plates. Miss Faber sat down across from Michael. "I can't believe how much you boys have grown! Seems like it was just yesterday I was handing you to your mama for the first time, Michael!"

Michael grinned. "I don't think anybody's gonna be handing me to her again!"

The group laughed. Lana turned to Dixie. "If you want, I think it would be okay to take Isaac and Lydia some dinner now. I'm sure they're ready for it." Miss Faber nodded in agreement.

The girls eagerly fixed a second tray of food and lemonade and took it upstairs to the waiting family. Annie knocked on the door. "Come in," Isaac called.

Annie held the door open for Dixie. Isaac and Lydia smiled as Isaac accepted the trays and set them on the bed. "Would you like to hold the baby, Dixie?" Lydia offered.

"Oh, I'd love to!" Dixie cradled the baby in her arms. "She's so precious! I just love babies!"

Lydia smiled. Isaac blessed their food and handed Lydia her plate.

Dixie asked, "What y'all gonna call her?"

The couple looked at each other. Isaac finally said, "We haven't decided yet. We know we want Elizabeth for the middle name, but the first name has us stumped. We'll just keep thinking. Any suggestions?"

Dixie and Annie looked at each other. Annie spoke first. "Cynthia flows with Elizabeth. That might work."

Isaac nodded. "True, but I have a cousin named Cynthia."

"Oh, I forgot the Williams were your cousins as well as Dixie's! Silly me. There goes that one."

Dixie knit her brow. "Sorry, I can't think of anything. I'm sure something will come to you. We'll be up in a few minutes to get your dishes." Reluctantly she handed the baby back to Isaac.

The girls headed for the door. "Thank y'all," Isaac said, cuddling his little girl in one arm and holding his cup in the other.

"She's so cute," Dixie exclaimed upon returning to the kitchen. Annie voiced her agreement. "I can't wait for y'all to see her!"

The boys looked at each other. They couldn't wait either, but right now their stomachs couldn't wait for the nice apple pie on the counter.

★1861★

Richard was surprised by the arrival of his little cousin, who was only a little over three hours old by the time he got home. Isaac brought her out into the hall so Richard could see her.

The baby looked like a china doll, so delicate that you would be afraid of breaking her. In looks, she favored the Mason side of the family. But she had chocolate brown hair like her mother.

Richard grinned as he looked at the baby. "Congratulations, Isaac. Looks like you've got yourself another title to add to the list, *Papa*."

Isaac grinned. "I wouldn't have it any other way. I suppose I should have joined the boys back in the fields, but I can't bring myself to leave my little family."

"Take the day off and any time you need and don't think about it. We can take care of the fields."

"Thanks. Oh, by the way, we finally decided on a name for the baby. Looks like you get to be the first to hear it."

"What is it?"

"Liberty."

Richard nodded approvingly. "Very fitting."

★ 1861 ★

"It's kinda funny," Tyler commented a few days later. "Liberty is a name you don't hear that much. But it's the perfect name for the present times. We *will* gain our Liberty! I just know it!"

This speech was directed to Seth, who was on his way to the post office. Seth smiled. "Yeah, I know what you mean"

As they entered the office, Seth was hoping for a letter from his parents announcing their return. Tyler had tagged along to see if his family had any mail.

Seth looked through the small stack of mail he received. Three letters...one from Aunt Pauline...one from Faye White, a friend of Dixie's...and one from where? Yes, this one was from England! Mama and Papa had written them!

As they headed back through town, Tyler asked, "Are you and Richard going to enlist if North Carolina secedes?"

Seth nodded. "We feel God leading us to. I personally hope the problem will be settled quickly. We decided to wait on

Papa and Mama to get back before we enlist. We want to talk with them about it first."

"That's a good idea. My parents have accepted that I'm enlisting, but they asked me to wait until North Carolina leaves the Union."

"Yeah, that's when I want to enlist. But if we don't secede before too long, I think me and Richard might go on up to Virginia to enlist anyway. I just can't stand the thought of tyranny in the 'Land of the Free.'"

"I know. The Yankees are our Egyptians. I'm just trying to figure out who our Moses is gonna be!"

★ 1861 ★

"Hey, Y'all, we got a…"

"Shhh!" Seth stopped mid-sentence. Everyone at the table had a finger pressed to his or her lips.

"What?" Seth whispered.

"Liberty just fell asleep. And if you wake her up, you'll get it!" Michael declared.

"Oh," Seth said nodding his head. "Uh, well, I have a letter here from…well you wouldn't care about it that much. I mean, why get excited about a letter from England?" he said teasingly.

Dixie squealed in delight and then clamped her hand over her mouth.

"Open it, Seth!" Richard said excitedly.

"Alright." He slit open the envelope, and then said innocently, "Should I read it out loud?"

"Seth! Just read it!" everyone said in unison.

"The letter reads:

Dear Children,   *April 1861*

We hope this letter finds everyone in good health. We miss y'all terribly, and can't wait to have

67

everyone together again. It rains almost every day here, which is a little tiresome, but we just remember that soon we'll be back in North Carolina.

We got our contract renewed, thank the Lord! Mr. Bennett was very kind and raised the price to one cent more per pound of cotton! That will certainly be a help to us. God is good!

Isaac and Lydia, we really appreciate your willingness to keep the house and work going in our absence. Without your help we certainly couldn't have made this trip.

Sorry to keep this letter so short. Children, we love and miss each of you and we are praying for y'all.

With love,
Papa and Mama
P.S. We return on the 30th of April. We booked passage for an early return. Praise the Lord!

"The 30th! That's next week! I can't wait!" exclaimed Michael.

Dixie smiled. "Me neither."

 ★1861★

Chapter 8

★

A Righteous Cause

*¹The LORD is my light and my salvation; whom shall I fear? the
LORD is the strength of my life; of whom shall I be afraid? ³Though
an host should encamp against me, my heart shall not fear: though
war should rise against me, in this will I be confident.*
Psalm 27:1&3

With gardening, chores and a new baby around the house,
the week went by quickly, and they once again found
themselves at the depot, this time awaiting the train's arrival.

"Mama! Papa! I'm so glad you're home!" Michael called,
reaching them first. Hugs were plenteous and Mama made sure
that each of her children received a kiss.

It was about 5:45 in the evening, so Richard was off
work and supper was ready at the house. Liberty was taking her
nap, so Lydia and Isaac had stayed home with her.

When they reached home, Lydia and Isaac greeted
everyone at the door. Isaac held Liberty, who had just awakened.
Of course Silas and Ellen had to hold their new grand-niece and
Isaac enjoyed showing her off.

After a delicious meal of chicken and dumplins, corn,
dried apples, and cornbread, they gathered in the back parlor to

talk…and talk…and talk. It was nearly midnight before they got to bed!

After breakfast the next morning, they had devotions and were soon saying farewell to Isaac, Lydia and Liberty. Then Dixie showed her parents her new stallion. She walked him out of the barn and around the yard.

"He's a beautiful stallion, Dixie! He's a good solid horse," Papa stated. Dixie smiled at her father's approval.

Mama stroked the horse's neck. "Does he have a name yet?" she inquired.

Dixie smiled and stroked her horse as she replied, "I'm gonna call him 'Confederate.' I thought it would be appropriate. His name was 'Boston,' but I knew that wouldn't work. He hasn't given me any trouble at all, but he's still a little timid. I think he'll outgrow that though. He's pretty playful. I couldn't dream of having a better horse."

"Can you ride him?" Papa asked.

"Yep. He was broken in when I got him. All I had to do was earn his trust. Watch," she said, hopping atop the gray horse, bareback. Grabbing a handful of his silky mane, she lightly pressed her heels into his sides. "Let's go, boy."

The horse quickly responded and started at a walk. Dixie worked him up to a canter then halted him and dismounted.

Mama was pleased with his quick obedience. Dixie rubbed him fondly. "I wrote Papa Rains a thank you note and told him the name I'd chosen. He wrote back and said he laughed when he heard the name, but he thought I'd named him well." Papa and Mama laughed. That was just like Papa Rains, never wanting to offend a grandchild, even if they didn't agree with his views.

Seth then took them inside the barn to see his mare. Rebel Lady whinnied in greeting when she saw Seth. Mama fell in love with the beautiful buckskin. She stroked her stomach gently. "Seth, she's got one big baby in there."

Seth laughed. "I know! I figure she's due soon, but I'm not an expert on horses."

Richard glanced at his pocket watch. "Oh, no! It's time for me to leave for the store! See y'all later."

★ 1861 ★

On May 3rd Abraham Lincoln called for over 42,000 army volunteers in addition to the ones he'd already called for in April. May 6th proved to be a very eventful day in the political realm. Arkansas seceded from the Union, and Lincoln made one of his biggest mistakes…

That afternoon Howard Wheeling rushed into the general store with interesting news. This news made everyone talk at once, and total confusion followed. What was this news? The Yankees had officially declared war on the Confederacy. How did Howard know this? He had overheard some bluecoats talking at the cafe.

Howard explained that shortly afterward a telegram for the newspaper office came announcing the same news. Richard's head dropped. Why? Why couldn't things have been worked out peacefully? He knew that war was coming, but that didn't mean he was prepared for it to start so soon.

"Well, if it's a fight over freedom, count me in!" declared one gentleman shopper. "Let the Second War of Independence begin."

"That's right! We must defend ourselves from the invaders of our liberties," another man agreed.

One young man shook his head. "But they ain't invading us! North Carolina's still in the Union!"

The men turned on the man with indignation. "What are you talking about? North Carolina's only in the Union by a thread! We'll come out before long, or I don't know our government leaders! Even if we weren't going to leave the union, it would be suicide not to! We'd be blocked in by Confederate states! But we *are* leaving the Union!"

Richard watched as the young man backed out of the store. That was probably best; someone may have furthered the argument if he hadn't.

Joel Lanier, a friend of Richard's, wrestled through the milling throng with a few items. "It's a mad house in here, Richard!" he said, placing his purchases on the counter.

"I know. You've heard the news?"

"Sure, who hasn't? It's spreading all around town. Mama's awful upset about it. She's already begged me not to go off. I told her I'd hold out for a while, but I still may go later."

Richard nodded, adding up Joel's bill. "It'll all be over before you'll have to go. It won't last a month when it comes to shots."

Joel shrugged. "Maybe. When Liberty's the objective, the oppressor won't give it cheaply. See you later."

"Bye."

Richard returned to stocking shelves, but he couldn't keep his mind on his work. Everyone coming into the store was talking and not buying. At last, Mr. Spencer told Richard there wasn't much reason to keep him there and gave him the rest of the day off.

Richard let Champion choose his pace as they started home. It gave him time to think. Freedom. Was that really what the states were going to fight over? Was Liberty the main objective?

Snatches of previous conversations flooded back to his memory. "*...The states have started seceding to protect their rights from being taken away. ... Well, think of it this way, the North are the British and we are the Patriots. That's the way it is. We are trying to gain our independence from Yankee tyranny.*" Richard remembered that discussion well. His father had been explaining secession to Michael.

Next came a conversation with his Uncle Robert Rains, whom he greatly admired. "*...Leaving the Union is ridiculous. It's like a child, upon finding he can't have a toy he wants, he throws all his other toys away. It is not just rebellious and foolish, but it makes the child sorry later...*"

Was the South acting like a bratty child? No! It wasn't! He knew his father was right. After all, if the Patriots had felt the way his uncle did, there wouldn't be Freedom to begin with.

Richard knew what the real question was. He and Seth had often discussed it. The question was, "What am *I* supposed to do?" Part of Richard said, "Don't do anything. North Carolina is still in the Union. Besides, why go and get yourself killed?" The other part said, "Don't just sit there and do nothing! You get out there and fight for what's right!"

Richard pulled on Champion's reins and dismounted. He knelt down beside the horse and prayed God would show him what to do. This wasn't the first time he had sought the Lord on this subject. But this time was different. It seemed as though God was pressing the answer on his heart.

When he mounted again, Richard knew what he was to do. He would defend what he knew was right. He would enlist in the Confederate Army. Richard knew receiving his parent's blessing wouldn't be a problem.

Yes, this was what God wanted. Richard was now prepared to defend his family, his country, and the righteous cause of Freedom.

★1861★

When Richard reached the barn to stable Champion, he found his father there too, getting some tools. "You're home early, son," Papa remarked.

"Yes, sir. Not much buying going on today."

Papa studied Richard's face. He could tell something was bothering his son. "What's wrong?"

Richard looked up at Papa in surprise. He sighed and looked out the barn door towards the house. At last he turned back to his father. "The Yankees have finally declared war on the Confederacy, Papa. It's official now. Guess there's no avoiding it."

Papa exhaled deeply. "Well, shots haven't been fired yet. Keep praying."

Richard nodded and remembered his new resolve to serve his country. He thought of Isaac and Lydia's baby, Liberty. If she could grow up free from Yankee tyranny, it would be worth all the pain and suffering he would go through during the war.

Papa set down his tools. "I suppose we should tell the others. I'd rather tell them myself than for them to find out secondhand."

Richard nodded and the two headed inside and found Mama in the back parlor sewing. Richard excused himself to change into field clothes and allow Papa and Mama some time alone.

When he returned, he found them sitting on the sofa. Mama was crying, and Papa was doing his best to comfort her. She looked up at her oldest son. His eyes reflected his concern. She smiled at him and squeezed her husband's hand.

"God will work it out, dear," Papa said softly. "He always has, and He will again."

A few minutes later, Papa and Richard left for the west pasture. Dixie had arrived ahead of them with cold water for the workers. *Now's as good a time as any to tell them,* Papa thought.

Tyler looked up and waved as Richard leaned up against the wagon. "You're home early," Michael commented, taking another sip of water.

"Yep, sure am."

Papa nodded. "Richard has some news."

All eyes turned to Richard. "What is it?" Dixie asked, concern in her voice.

Richard looked over the group of anxious listeners. "Howard Wheeling told us that Lincoln has formally and officially declared war on the Confederacy. America's going to war once again."

Silence reigned. Tyler and Seth looked at each other with knowing glances. Dixie sat down on the edge of the wagon bed, stunned by the announcement. Papa walked over to her and placed an arm around her.

Michael broke the silence with, "Well, at least we didn't start it! They can't blame that on us."

Everyone turned to look at Michael, who was haply perched on a wagon wheel. "What? It's true. This way, they'll go down in history as tyrants and invaders."

A nervous laugh rippled through the group. Dixie quickly left the field. Her heart was heavy with the blow. She was still trying to comprehend what was happening as she entered the house.

She found Mama in the parlor. She looked up when Dixie walked in. "You've heard?" Mama asked, tears in her eyes.

"It's terrible!" Dixie gasped before bursting into tears. Mama left her mending, and the two hugged each other tightly, crying on each other's shoulder. The trouble had at last begun.

★ 1861 ★

Not long after war had been declared, Richard asked if Papa and Mama could talk with him and Seth in the study. Papa had an idea of what they wanted to talk about, and even though he had peace about it, he still had a twinge of sadness deep inside.

Once they reached the study, Papa had everyone sit down. Mama, too, had a suspicion as to the reason of the meeting. After everyone was seated, Papa said as calmly as he could, "Boys, what's on your minds?"

Richard spoke first. "Papa, you and Mama always taught us that when we feel we need to make a decision, we should pray first and see what God wants." Papa nodded.

Richard slowly continued. "We've been doing that. And…" he paused and took a deep breath. "We believe that God wants us to join the Confederate Army." He absentmindedly bit his lower lip. Seth was watching his parents, trying to decipher their reaction.

Papa drew a deep breath and unshed tears glistened in Mama's eyes. Richard wasn't sure if that meant they were upset or if they were just sad. Papa tried to say something, but hesitated.

Finally, Papa found his voice. "Boys, I'm proud of you. It's just all the 'what-ifs' that can get in the way sometimes. Your mother and I have discussed and prayed about it, just in case God laid it on your hearts. You're sure this is God's will and not your own desires?"

"It would have to be God telling me to go," Seth said quickly. "I'd much rather be here working with you on the plantation. But I keep thinking about Great-grandpa Mason being a Patriot and risking it all to gain Independence for this country. I feel I need to do the same to regain that Freedom. I've prayed about it and I do believe it's God's will."

"What about you, Richard?" Papa asked, placing his arm around Mama.

Richard didn't hesitate. "I'm fighting for three reasons. First and foremost, I'm fighting because, as I told you, I believe God wants me to. I want to be a witness to our soldiers as well. Second, I want my family to be free of Union oppression. I don't want Dixie and Michael to grow up in a place where they don't have the freedom to live the way their ancestors have lived for years. They should have the right to choose how they live as long as it lines up with the Bible. I want to protect my family from tyranny.

"Thirdly, I'm fighting because I want to retain my rights. I believe the states are stronger united, but I also believe that it is wrong for one group of people to intimidate and force their ideas on another. This is why I feel I must fight."

Mama wanted to cry, but instead she was breathing through it. Papa and Mama were proud of their sons' convictions and the stand they were taking to protect what mattered the most to them.

"Boys, I am so proud of y'all. Sounds like y'all prayed and thought this thing through. But remember, North Carolina is still in the Union; she may not secede," Papa added.

The brothers looked at each other and Richard nodded. Seth said, "Papa, I know North Carolina is our home, but this isn't a decision made by each state; this is a decision made by each man. We want to go up to Virginia and enlist there. They've already seceded and will be raising an army soon, and we want to join their ranks."

Silas studied his two sons for a moment. "Do you already have a date in mind that you want to leave?"

"We'd like to head out on the 17th," Richard began. "With the war officially on, who knows when Lincoln's army will attack? They need men, and they'll need them fast. This war won't last long once it comes to the fighting. And the Yanks need to see our loyalty. We need to overwhelm them with our numbers. But if you say wait, then we'll wait."

Mama hadn't really heard the last bit of what Richard had said; she was stuck on the departure date. "Next Friday," she whispered. "So soon..." Mama sighed and looked out the window for a moment to keep her composure.

Silas smiled broadly. "That's a fine word, son: loyalty. I'll never meet two finer young men to carry out the meaning of that word. And I'm not gonna let your loyalty to me stand in the way of what you already know you need to do. If the 17th is the day you need to leave, then we should be able to make that happen, right Ellen?"

"I suppose we can make preparations in time," she said reluctantly, her voice quivering a little. "But we'll have to start right away."

"Then it's settled," Papa said. "Y'all leave next Friday."

At last, Mama could hold back her tears no longer. She stood and walked over to the window. After a few moments, Papa went over and whispered something to her.

She nodded and took a deep breath. Then she and Papa walked over to the boys and hugged them, telling the boys how proud they were of them. They talked a while longer then ended with a prayer of protection and blessing on their brave boys.

★ 1861 ★

Chapter 9
★
The First Good-Bye

Some trust in chariots, and some in horses: but we will remember the
name of the LORD our God.
Psalm 20:7

The week had been a blur for the Mason family. Mama had a list of things that had to be done before Richard and Seth left for Virginia. Dixie had been assigned to making sure the clothes they were taking were in top notch condition. Michael was the errand boy, running around the house and back and forth to town to pick up anything Mama and Mrs. Bradley needed.

Upon hearing about the boys' departure, the Naces had allowed Tyler to go along with them instead of waiting on the North Carolina legislature to take action. He would be with people he knew, and that was comforting to his family. The party soon grew to four when Richard and Seth's cousin Jordan Williams decided to go ahead and enlist as well.

It was Thursday evening now, and with their lists completed, the Masons could relax. They were at Pastor Brewster's house, along with the Naces and Williams for a farewell gathering. The families were there for supper, and Lana was finally going to tell her "Sumter story!" Everyone was excited, because for some reason the newspaper had only given a brief account about the conflict. Jordan's sisters Alexandria and Cynthia sat on either side of their big brother. Alyssa Rose sat on Tyler's lap playing with a doll while the older ones listened.

After everyone was situated, Pastor Brewster said, "We're so glad everyone was able to gather with us this evening. We've been looking forward to sharing our firsthand account of the victory at Ft. Sumter. If y'all don't mind, Lana's gonna tell the story, since she and the cousins experienced more of the excitement than us adults."

A hush fell over the group as Lana began. "As y'all know, we were visiting family in South Carolina. It was early in the morning, and I was asleep. Then, about 4:30, I woke up to a cannon firing off nearby. I jumped out of bed and ran downstairs with my cousin, Faye. We looked out the window and saw lights and soldiers and cannons facing Fort Sumter." Lana's face flushed as she continued. "Then we screamed. I do believe Papa thought someone was trying to kill us!" Everyone laughed.

"One thing's for sure. We woke up everyone who hadn't been awakened by the cannons. That would be the boys." Again everyone laughed, as Dixie cast an accusing look at Michael who could sleep through anything.

"Before long, everyone was peering out the window toward the water. We heard cannon ball after cannon ball hit the fort. They were so close to the house that we had to take all the pictures down off the walls. Three had broken due to the vibrations.

"We all started praying that no one would be hurt. Then we got dressed. No one was very hungry, so we skipped breakfast. Chores in the barn couldn't be neglected, so the boys ran to the barn. It was kinda funny. You would have thought there were cannons firing at them, but I don't think they were in any danger.

"At dinner, Uncle Mark and Jacob decided to go to town and send some telegrams. They continued to fire all day. None of us slept well that night. The next day they were still at it. Papa,

Uncle Mark, Jacob and Luke carefully made their way to one of the Confederate positions to make sure it was safe for us to remain at the house.

"They spoke with one of the officers and returned. The officer said it looked like we were safe and that they, the Confederates, were about to take the fort. And sure enough a little later, we ran outside to watch as the Union flag came down and the white one went up. We cheered and clapped with others who were watching.

"At the official surrender, the Yankees were allowed to fire a 100 gun salute. One gun went off too soon and killed a Union soldier. He was the only one killed during the whole fight." Dixie and Annie gasped.

Lana told them of the celebrations that took place. "The boys got to meet some of the Confederate soldiers, and I'm positive that I saw our own Sheriff Gallimore there too."

Questions about details were asked and excited conversation followed. The families parted after Pastor Brewster prayed a special prayer for the southern military and for the boys, who were leaving for war the next day.

★ 1861 ★

Dixie's face was streaked with tears as she hugged Seth. She then turned to Richard, who hugged her tightly. Michael didn't say much at all. His room was going to feel very empty in his brothers' absence. They would soon be boarding the train that would take them to Virginia.

Leaving their family for war was the hardest thing Richard and Seth had ever done, and now the time had come. After Papa led the family in prayer for the boys' protection and well-being, Mama gave them one last long embrace. Then the boys boarded the train and waved goodbye to their family until they couldn't see them anymore.

Richard watched as Seth settled into his seat. Seth wouldn't look up at his older brother. He just stared at the floor.

He always got quiet when he was bothered by something. Jordan and Tyler sat across the aisle from them.

One of the young men sitting in front of them turned around and spoke solemnly yet sincerely. "It was nice of your folks to see you off. You all must be a very close family. I can't imagine my family coming to see me off."

Richard shook his head. "They didn't come see you off?"

"Nope, I said goodbye at the house. My little sister came with me, but she left right before you got here." Richard and Seth looked at each other and back at the boy.

"I'm sorry to hear that." Richard said. It was hard for him to imagine his parents not caring about him leaving for war. It was such a pity!

"Oh, pardon me. My name is Jeremiah Calling, but some people call me Jeremy. I'm seventeen and I am from Southern Maryland. I've lived in North Carolina for the past year, and I aim to defend her from any and all adversities."

"That's adversaries, crazy," said the young man next to him. "I'm Alvin Willis. I'm Jeremy's neighbor."

"I'm Richard Mason and this is my brother, Seth. Over there is our cousin Jordan Williams and our friend, Tyler Nace."

"Nice to meet y'all," Alvin said. The boys all shook hands.

"So, do any of you have horses?" Jeremy asked. Seth was taken aback by the sudden change of subject, so Richard responded.

"Yeah, we both do. I have a brown stallion and Seth has a buckskin mare. I brought Champion, but Seth left Lady behind 'cause she's about to foal." Tyler and Jordan described their horses as well.

Alvin looked over at Seth. "You're a quiet one aren't you?" he teased.

Seth smiled and nodded. Richard grinned. "He's not like that with people he knows," he said, playfully elbowing Seth. "He'll come around."

Jeremy asked them question after question. Before they realized it, they were in Virginia. The first thing the boys did was to find a recruiting station. That wasn't hard; they were everywhere.

When their turn came, Jordan asked, "Sir, do you have to be eighteen to enlist as a soldier? I know the United States Army has that requirement."

"Oh," the recruiter said with a wave of his hand, "If we followed that, we'd have more musicians than soldiers. How old are you?"

"Seventeen."

The recruiter nodded. "As long as you ain't a youngster, you can choose."

Jordan nodded and decided to go in for the soldiering. Tyler and Seth followed his example. The recruiter had them sign the roll for the company they were joining. He then had them raise their right hands and take a vow of allegiance.

"Alright, boys, your company is under Col. Thomas Jackson[8]. You'll leave tomorrow morning to head for his training ground. Now, go to town hall and you can pick up your gear there."

Once at town hall, the boys were given a cartridge box, a cap box, canteens, tin cups, haversacks and a few other items. They were asked if they had brought guns with them and if so, what model. Seth and Tyler didn't, so they were issued Enfield rifles.

Seth was quiet on the way to the makeshift camp. *We're really going,* he thought. *Really and truly going.*

★ 1861 ★

When they arrived at the campsite the next day, they were briefed on who their superiors were, how and when to

---

[8] Former teacher at the Virginia Military Institute and the Hero of Manassas Junction! His resolve and faith in God led to the miraculous victory in Virginia.

salute, and which tent they were to stay in. By the end of the day the boys' heads were spinning.

The next day they were awakened at 4:00 by a shrill bugle call.

By 6:30 everyone was ready for drilling. By the end of the day everyone was ready for a break. Richard and Seth agreed that military life was very different from plantation life.

They felt a little out of place with all the Virginia Military Institute (VMI) students, but they were friendly and helped the boys learn all the proper military lingo.

That night, Richard wrote a letter home. He closed it with, *I miss y'all terribly. I can't wait to see you again. (Yes I'm homesick even though I've only been gone a few days!) Love, from your son/brother, Richard.*

★ 1861 ★

Dixie and Michael kept close tabs on everything that was going on in the newspaper, especially now that war was on and their brothers were in it. On the 7th of May Tennessee, in effect, seceded by becoming allies with the Confederacy.

The recruitment of 400,000 Confederate soldiers had been authorized on the 16th. Then North Carolina had seceded on the 20th. The boys had missed it by three days, but it didn't matter. They had a head start on their fellow North Carolinians as far as training went.

The Confederacy had moved their capital from Montgomery, Alabama to Richmond, Virginia. This change made the North angry. The "Rebel" capital being that close to their own, they felt, was an insult.

On the 24th of May, federal troops began the invasion of the South by entering Virginia and occupying Alexandria. To further gain a foothold in the South, they pressed on and took Newport News.

At last, shots had been fired in June. The clash of arms took place at Big Bethel, Va. and had ended in Confederate victory. But as of yet, Richard and Seth had seen no action; just drill, drill and more drill.

★ 1861 ★

By June, Richard and Seth had been assigned to the 1st Virginia Brigade, 2nd Virginia Regiment. July 2nd and 3rd, a small group of the 1st Virginia were caught up in a skirmish with the enemy, but because of orders from higher ranking officers, Jackson slowly withdrew his men without routing the enemy.

For his expert conduct during the fight and obedience to orders, Col. Jackson received a promotion to Brigadier General. Richard and Seth were not involved in this affair though they were prepared to fight if they had to.

One evening Richard carefully cleaned out the barrel of his rifle. "Has anyone ever asked you if you were kin to Mr. Lincoln in Washington?"

Richard looked up from his work and saw a VMI cadet standing in front of him. "Nope, can't say as they have. What makes you ask that?"

"You're certainly tall enough for the part! How tall are you?"

Richard shrugged. "Six foot something. I guess it don't seem that fantastic to me, 'cause just about every man in my family's tall."

The cadet smiled and stuck out his hand. "Cpl. Titus Mallory," he introduced himself.

Richard shook hands with Cpl. Mallory. "Pvt. Richard Mason. It's good to meet you."

"Likewise. Now I can tell from how you talk you're not from around here. Where's home for you?"

"Four Tree Springs, North Carolina. It's in the middle of the state."

Titus nodded. "North Carolina, alright. You're not too far from home. So, how'd the town end up with a name like Four Tree Springs? There must be a story behind it."

84

Richard laughed. "Oh, there's a story behind it alright. My ancestors came down to North Carolina back in the late 1600's and made their home with a Cherokee Indian tribe. Because of their friendship, the tribe gave them the land where our town now stands. The name came from a little natural spring at the base of Mt. Dogwood. It's not exactly a mountain, but it's big so we call it a mountain. But anyway, the spring had four different trees growing near it; a dogwood, an oak, a pine, and a poplar. So that's how the name came about."

"That's really interesting. I doubt my hometown has a history like that! I might just look into it," Titus said. "The reason I came over here is that my sergeant asked me to teach you a few thing about our brigade. I know you've learned a lot, but one thing you should know about is our special yell."

"Your what?"

For a reply, Titus, at the top of his lungs, shouted, "Woh-who-ey!"

Richard's response was, "What are you supposed to be? A wildcat or an Indian?"

Titus laughed. "We're gonna do that when we charge the enemy. You'd better learn it too. It's supposed to scare them."

"I think it's effective," Richard agreed. "It's terrifying!"

★ 1861 ★

"Alright men, break camp. We're heading out. Come on, come on, let's go!" the sergeants yelled early one morning in late July. "We're heading out! Move it, let's go!"

Richard and Seth jumped up from their breakfast and prepared to leave. They quickly packed their things into their haversacks. Half an hour later, the camp was packed up and heading out.

If the soldiers had known what the next few days held in store for them, they would have been dragging their feet. Oh, they knew a fight was coming, but they didn't fully realize what was about to happen. The name Manassas Junction[9] would be forever etched in their minds.

 ★1861★

---

[9] Manassas Junction, Va. is the site of the first major battle of the Civil War. (AKA the First Battle of Bull Run.)

Chapter 10

★

The Awakening

Thou therefore endure hardness, as a good soldier of Jesus Christ.
II Timothy 2:3

"Then, Sir, we will give them the bayonet!"
General Thomas Jonathan Jackson

"Move on in, boys. Don't worry about comfort, just crowd on in." Richard and Seth quickly scrambled into the train car in front of them. Tyler and Jordan were right behind them. It didn't take long for the car to fill up.

Richard glanced over at Seth who was standing with his head leaned against the wall of the car. "You alright?"

Seth nodded. "It's a little crowded in here. As long as I don't look around, I'm fine."

"Alright."

Suddenly the train lurched forward, knocking soldiers into each other. Seth regained his balance and stared hard at the wall. *I'm alright, I am alright,* he said to himself.

Before too long Seth was able to look around and not feel too closed in or sick. He pulled out his pocket Bible and turned to Luke where he'd been reading. Tyler looked over his shoulder and read along with him. Richard glanced at Jordan and laughed; he'd fallen asleep, leaning in the corner of the car.

Sweat trickled down Richard's face. It was certainly hot in the cars. He took off his hat and vainly tried to fan himself without hitting other people. His height helped some, but not enough. Seth glanced up at his brother and grinned. Richard's hair was soaked. Then again, his probably was too. He was surely looking forward to getting some fresh air.

★ 1861 ★

July 21st, 1861, near Manassas Junction, Virginia, General P.G.T. Beauregard[10] was about to engage in the first major battle of the war.

"Here they come!"

"Form ranks!"

"Prepare for battle!"

The Yankees were on their way. After receiving word from a Confederate spy, the Confederates sent for reinforcements. The Confederates were outnumbered around 30,000 to 23,000.

The Confederates laughed as they saw several Yankees break out of line to pick berries from well stocked bushes. "Look at them dandies! Sure do have a lot of discipline. They're so polite to leave the bushes there instead of taking them along with them!" one said sarcastically.

"Well, it makes good war paint!" joked another soldier. He was using field glasses and passed them around so the others could see. He pointed to one Yankee who had obviously got berry juice on his hands and had perhaps scratched his nose, for he now had the juice smeared across it! It was nearly impossible to suppress the laughter as each soldier took a look through the field glasses.

---

[10] Hero of Ft. Sumter; received official surrender from his former teacher, Robert Anderson.

But their laughter wouldn't last long. They had a battle to fight in mere moments.

★ 1861 ★

Dixie sat in the living room, reading some Psalms. Papa and Mama had retired to their room and Michael was coming downstairs at that moment.

"I'm gonna check on Lady, alright?" he called to Dixie, referring to Seth's mare. She was near to delivering, so Michael was keeping an eye on her.

Dixie was finishing up Psalm 5 when Michael raced back into the sitting room. "Dixie! It's coming! I can see it! Mr. Bradley said it won't be long. He's with her now. Come on, hurry!" With that, he ran back out to the barn with Dixie close behind him.

As they entered the barn, Lady gave a weak nicker of greeting. *Poor thing, she sounds like she's worn out!* Dixie thought. Dixie entered the stall, and sure enough, she was in labor. Only the hind legs were left to be born. Dixie rubbed Lady's neck. "Michael, get Papa," she said softly.

By the time they got there, the dark, blue gray colored colt was born. He had a dorsal stripe like his parents, as well as a white stripe on his nose.

They waited for Lady to get her strength and tend to her new baby. But she didn't show any signs of getting up at all. Her eyes were closed and her breathing was labored. Then she began to push again.

Mr. Bradley knit his brow and leaned over to feel Lady's stomach. His suspicion was confirmed; there was another baby in there. "Children, dry off the foal. Lady's got a little more work to do."

Silas studied Mr. Bradley's face. He knew the risks involved in a horse delivering twins. It was very probable that Lady or the foals or all three could die. He knew how much Seth would miss Lady. But there was nothing they could do. They could only wait and see what happened.

89

★ 1861 ★

Mr. and Mrs. Nace were sitting in Pastor Brewster's study. They were there to discuss Tyler with the pastor, who, you may remember, was Mrs. Nace's brother. Tyler had seemed so troubled the day he'd left for Virginia.

"I just can't figure out what's troubling him," Jonathan began. "Moving here has improved his people skills, but he still seems so troubled."

Pastor Brewster sat back in his chair. "Do you know around when this started?"

Jonathan and Kathie looked at each other. Suddenly, Kathie's eyes lit up. "October, remember, when the Thatcher's came to our church from out west. They were giving an update on their ministry to the Indians."

"That's right," Jonathan agreed. "Do you think there's a connection there?"

Pastor Brewster shrugged. "Could be. Did this family make any negative impressions on Tyler?"

"Oh, no," Kathie said quickly. "They are a precious family. Tyler was impressed with them, especially their son, James. He said he was surprised someone so young could take such a big part in his father's ministry."

"Hmmm…" Pastor Brewster said, toying with the end of his mustache. "What part has Tyler taken in Christian service?"

Again, the couple looked at each other. Jonathan furrowed his brow. "I suppose none at all," he admitted. "He attended all church meetings with us and of course tithed off his earnings. But beyond that, nothing that I know of."

Pastor Brewster nodded. "That could be it. Perhaps this James Thatcher you spoke of has awakened a sense of neglected duty in Tyler. You said the young man impressed him. Maybe Tyler has discovered how little he has done for his Savior."

"That would make sense," Jonathan said, catching his wife's eye. She nodded in agreement. "That makes a lot of sense."

It wasn't until 12:00 that afternoon that Jackson's men reached the field. They heard the battle begin long before it reached them. The sound was terrifying. Seth shook his head. "Maybe they won't come back this far."

The Yankees didn't come back that far...until around 2:00 that afternoon. Seth saw them; blue uniforms, shiny guns and detonating bullets. The drums pounded, and guns and cannons boomed loudly. Seth was glad he had cotton in his ears, or he was sure he would be deaf!

The battle raged on. The Yanks kept pushing the Confederates back to "Henry Hill." The high ground was still in Confederate hands, but they were holding by a thread. If they lost the hill...they would lose this battle.

Jackson moved his troops to a pine glen and ordered a nine gun artillery force. General J.E.B. "Jeb" Stuart's[11] Calvary was then positioned at General Jackson's left flank. The Yankees started flooding them with artillery fire.

Jackson and his men were positioned near a creek called Bull Run. Some of the soldiers said that whichever side called retreat would be the "Bull Runners!" Everyone liked that and purposed that they wouldn't be the retreating force.

Seth heard from another soldier that several well-dressed families were there to watch the battle with their dinner. This made Seth's blood boil. The very idea of watching men fight and die as entertainment was preposterous! It was downright sinful!

"Instruct the men to lie down!" General Jackson ordered. Even though the Masons had never heard of the man before they joined the army, they knew there was something about him that set him apart from the others. He seemed to know everything would turn out alright in the end.

"1st rank lay down! 2nd rank, kneel!"

---

[11] Confederate Cavalry officer. James Ewell Brown Stuart is his proper name.

Richard prayed as he checked over his gun. Seth was kneeling next to him. "Seth, I want you to stay away from me during the fighting. If one of those cannons comes through here…anyway, we'd better put some space between us."

For the first time, the reality that they may not make it home was forced to the front. Seth looked at his brother. "What ifs" whirled through his mind, but he slowly nodded and moved further down the line. He pushed away the thought that he may have just seen Richard for the last time.

Seth and Tyler found themselves kneeling side by side. Tyler began the tedious loading process. He took a cartridge out of his cartridge bag, and bit off the paper end of the cartridge, holding the bullet between his teeth.

He poured the gunpowder down the muzzle of the gun, took the bullet out of his mouth and set it just inside the muzzle of his gun. He then pulled out his ramrod and forced the bullet and powder all the way down the barrel of the gun.

He raised the gun to chest height, and took a percussion cap out of a small pouch on his belt. The percussion cap was used to ignite the powder when the hammer of the gun struck it. He placed the cap on the cone, the metal piece that held the cap in place. He then lifted the gun, pulling it tight against his shoulder. He was now prepared to fire when the order was given. This process took some time.

The 2nd and 33rd Virginia Regiments were stationed to the left part of Jackson's army. They were positioned just below the crest of the hill. Perhaps they would charge soon…

★ 1861 ★

"It doesn't look good, Dixie," Papa said dolefully. Dixie gently stroked the light gray colt. He was smaller than his older twin and Papa had to assist Mr. Bradley in the delivery. Lady seemed fine, but she wouldn't feed the new colt. He kept making soft and weak cries for food.

Mr. Bradley suddenly had an idea. "When Dr. Wilmore's mare wouldn't feed her baby, he gave it cow's milk. I think he might have mixed some water with it."

"Can we try it, Papa?" Dixie asked, a glimmer of hope shining in her eyes. Silas was doubtful but gave his consent. Dixie flew into action. "Michael, get me a glass bottle."

"Alright."

Dixie ran inside and asked Mrs. Bradley to heat some milk from that morning's milking. It seemed to take forever for the milk to heat enough for the colt to drink. Finally, Dixie returned to the barn with a small pot of warm milk.

Michael handed her the bottle, and Dixie quickly poured the milk into it. *Dear Lord, please let this work,* Dixie prayed as Papa poured some lukewarm water into the milk. Dixie covered the hole with her hand and shook it to mix the water with the milk.

At first, the colt just held the milk in his mouth. Then, he gulped it down. They fed him a few more mouthfuls.

He then struggled to his feet, took two halting steps toward Lady, and whinnied. Lady turned toward him and sniffed him. She snorted and turned her back toward him. But this little guy refused to be ignored. He stomped his hooves and whinnied so loud that Lady jumped. The Masons laughed as the colt strode right up to Lady and began nursing.

Papa was amazed. "Maybe that little fighter's gonna make it! If he makes it through the night, I'd say he'll pull through."

★ 1861 ★

"They're gonna' break the line!"

"We can't hold them back much longer!"

"Stand your ground, men!"

The Union was indeed about to break the lines which would result in a Confederate retreat.

"Look, men! There is Jackson standing like a stone wall! Let us determine to die here and we will conquer." shouted

General Bernard Bee[12]. Several turned to look at the brave General Jackson and his men.

"Rally behind the Virginians!"

The Confederates banded together, but the Yankees were persistent. Some of Jackson's units were coming under fire, such as the 33rd Virginia under Col. A.C. Cumming[13]. Being next to the 2nd Virginia regiment, it was no surprise that they too were coming under fire.

Seth was reloading his gun when one of the officers remarked, "Cumming's men are charging! They'll be butchered!"

The boy's eyes widened as the unit charged, capturing an artillery position. But the unit didn't have enough men to hold the position. They were repelled by the Union front and were soon retreating.

Before long, orders arrived from their commander: "Counter attack with bayonets!" and "Reserve your fire until they come within fifty yards. Then fire and give them the bayonet." He also ordered them to yell with all their might.

Richard looked over at Jordan, who shrugged. "CHARGE BAYONETS!" The next thing the Yankees knew there were Confederates charging them, screaming at the top of their lungs...with bayonets!

Tyler rushed forward, bayonet extended toward the mass of Union soldiers. Few soldiers resisted the urge to run from the Confederates. But some did and because of them, Tyler prayed silently, *Lord let me live to see the end of this day!*

"I surrender!"

Tyler looked up in surprise. Seth had a Yankee artillerist backed up against the cannon with his blade pointed at the man's throat. Seth's eyes were ablaze with passion. He removed the

---

[12] Famous for giving Stonewall Jackson his nickname, Gen. Bee was killed shortly after his rousing speech.

[13] Col. Cumming was commander of the 33rd Virginia Regiment and ordered the charge when some of his men left the ranks and began to charge on their own.

point as the soldier dropped the pistol he had been pointing at Tyler.

Seth didn't take his eyes off the enemy soldier. "Tyler, you need to keep your eyes open if you're gonna pray on the field. This Yank just about took you out of here."

The reality of what Seth had said hit Tyler; he'd nearly been shot. Seth grabbed the soldier by the arm and forced him back towards the Confederate lines.

★ 1861 ★

"Retreat! Retreat!" The Confederates chased the Yankees across the field, still giving their ferocious "Rebel yell."

"Whoopee!" shouted a Confederate captain. "Let them have it, boys! Let them Bull Runners have it!"

Jordan looked over at Richard and grinned. "Well, at least *we* weren't the Bull Runners!" Richard smiled and let out a loud whoop with the others.

Confederate reinforcements soon arrived and followed up the attack on the Union's right flank. Shortly before 5:00 on the evening of July 21, 1861, Union General Irvin McDowell[14] admitted defeat and ordered a retreat. His men were more than willing to comply!

The Yankees ran as fast as their legs could carry them. The onlookers ran just as fast, causing a chaotic mass of soldiers and carriages.

The Confederates cheered their victory. Many threw their hats into the air. Richard immediately began to look for Seth. He eventually ended up back at the campsite, still searching.

He found his younger brother guarding prisoners with some other soldiers. Relief washed over Richard; they had both made it out of their first battle alive.

---

[14] Irvin McDowell led the Union forces at Manassas, but was relieved of his command in September of 1862 at the age of 43.

Meanwhile, Tyler was still on the battle field, staring at the scene of mass destruction. Had they really just done that? Had they really just won the battle? It all felt like a dream.

Once again he thought of his close encounter. He'd come that close to never seeing his family again. His stomach felt like one big knot. Just like that, he could have never again heard his father's strong voice or felt his mother's tender embrace. No more teasing Annie or fishing with Carter. No more holding little Alyssa Rose or telling her bedtime stories.

He sank to his knees. It seemed God was saying to him, "I've spared you twice, My son; once in sending My Son to die for your sins, which you've accepted. And this time by allowing your friend to shield you from a bullet. If I can do that for you, can you not live for Me and serve Me with your whole life?"

"Oh, Heavenly Father, forgive me! Forgive me for not serving You the way I should. Forgive me for letting others do Your work alone. Help me to be one of Your faithful servants, Father. Thank You for sparing me once again, Lord…"

When Tyler rose from his knees, he felt as if a heavy burden had been lifted from his shoulders. For the first time in months, he felt as if he were where he was supposed to be with God. He was at peace.

★ 1861 ★

A knock came at the front door the next morning at breakfast time. Mama answered it. "Oh, Pastor Brewster, Lana, come on in." She turned toward the dining room. "Silas, Pastor's here."

Greetings were exchanged and the Brewsters were invited to join them for breakfast. They declined, having already dined. Pastor Brewster looked rather grave. He handed Silas a telegram. "I thought you should see this."

Silas read the note aloud.

"Pastor A. Brewster: Battle yesterday at Manassas Junction, VA. Pray. Many casualties. G.G. Tremain."

Michael's face was pale. "Papa, may I be excused?"

"Of course, son." Michael hurried to his room.

"Who's G.G. Tremain?" Silas asked.

"Gabriel Tremain is a preacher friend of mine. He and his family actually live in Louisiana, but their oldest daughter is married and lives in Virginia. That's how they knew about the battle."

"I see."

★ 1861 ★

Michael sat in his room by himself for a while. Later, Dixie knocked on his door. "Come in."

She entered and sat on the edge of Seth's bed. At last, she spoke. "The telegram didn't say anything about Richard and Seth."

Michael looked over at her. "Mr. Tremain doesn't know us. Of course he wouldn't mention them."

Dixie sighed. "I know. I was just trying to look at the bright side."

"What bright side? In war, there is no bright side. Papa says hardly anyone escapes without getting hurt."

"Michael," she said, coming over and placing her hand on his shoulder, "you knew they would go to battle eventually. The sooner the fighting starts, the sooner it will all be over."

"Dixie, this is going to be a long one. Sure some Yanks ain't that bright, but they ain't gonna stop because we took one fort. We don't know who won this one yet; Mr. Tremain didn't say. Dixie, you're just too optimistic! No wonder Seth calls you 'Miss Optimism!' No, this is going to be a long one. I think this war will last a few years. No one ever gives in that easily. No one. Call me crazy if you want, but I truly believe that."

"I don't think you're crazy, Michael, but I don't believe you. This war will end soon," Dixie said softly. Tears swam in her eyes. But deep down, Dixie feared Michael was right. Their talk had made the reality of war sink in a little deeper. He was turned away from her now, but Dixie could tell he was really upset. They both missed their brothers, and the idea of any harm coming to them scared them both.

"Michael, why don't we pray right here and now. Richard, Seth, Cousin Jordan and…well, the whole Confederate military needs prayer right now."

"Sure, why not." So together they knelt in the boys' room to pray. I'm sure God looked down on them with tender love for their concerns.

 ★ 1861 ★

Chapter 11
★
Reality of War

Tyler walked slowly back to his tent, still remembering the scenes of the previous day's fight. He heard laughter coming from inside, and when he entered, Seth was "scolding," Richard. The two noticed Tyler's sober face and immediately ceased their bantering.

"What's wrong, Tyler?" Seth ventured.

Tyler slowly replied, "I just got the figures. Somewhere around 380 of our men are dead, 'bout 1,580 wounded and 13 missing. Those are the rough numbers." He swallowed. "I knew war was awful, but…"

"But you didn't know it would be this bad," Richard finished for him. Tyler nodded in agreement. Richard asked him, "What about our brigade? What're the 1st Virginia's losses?"

Tyler closed his eyes trying to remember the numbers. "111 dead, 373 wounded or missing. That's what I overheard, but there may be more. I don't know. I went with a burial detail, and…it was just awful. Dead and wounded everywhere and some were, um…well, they weren't all there." Richard's eyebrows arched and Seth shook his head.

Tyler hadn't finished. "Some are just little boys. One didn't look any older than my brother Carter, a drummer I guess. He was hurt bad and kept calling for his mama. I carried him to the doctor, but he died before the doctor got a chance to treat him. He died in my arms. I … I don't understand…"

Tyler couldn't finish. All he could think about was the little boy and his family. What if that had been Carter? How would he feel if he got news of his brother dying, calling for his mother and not getting to see her? The very thought made him feel sick.

The brothers who had been picking with each other only minutes before were very somber now. "I don't know what I would do if that were Michael," Seth said. "I think I'd go crazy."

"If only there were more doctors and nurses, he might have lived," sighed Tyler.

"Too bad Mama and Dixie aren't here, or even Lana. They could at least keep the doctors from being overworked. That in itself would be an improvement," Richard said, half to himself, half out loud.

"Yep, sure would be," Tyler agreed.

Richard sighed. "Too bad we can't get them here…or could we…?"

The three sat there in silence for a few moments. Knowing something needed to be said to brighten the mood, Richard said, "Seth, what was it you were saying before Tyler came in here?"

Seth caught the hint in his brother's voice. "I was saying you are one of the most careless and inconsiderate people in this camp. Your conduct is inexcusable!"

Tyler looked quizzically at his two friends. "What happened?" he asked Richard.

Richard opened his mouth to speak in his own defense, but Seth beat him to the explanation. "Richard has misplaced one of our most valuable possessions...our straight razor!"

Tyler stared at Richard trying to catch his mood. "Yeah, I lost mine too. I reckon we're all destined to have whiskers!"

"NO!" Seth said as though the very thought was going to make him sick. "I'm too young for that!"

A smile played around Tyler's lips as he pictured them all with whiskers. The boys laughed and kept up the good natured teasing a little longer before having to part for one reason or another.

★ 1861 ★

"Well, Dixie, I think that little feller's gonna do just fine. He's much stronger than yesterday."

Dixie smiled at her father. "Gray," as they had took to calling the colt, was still kind of weak, but was already frisking around the pasture. The colt avoided his older and much bossier brother.

"Blue," kept nipping at Gray until he could take no more. Gray whirled around, whinnying as loud as he could, and started chasing a very frightened Blue around the pasture.

The Masons laughed as Blue hid between his mother and father. Gray was very pleased with himself. He began prancing around as if to flaunt his victory. Mama shook her head and laughed a little harder.

"You know, those two make me think of the Yankees and the Confederates. The Yanks kept 'nipping' at us until we fought back!" Michael said.

"I hope Seth chooses different names for them. And I hope they don't stay at each other forever," Mama commented.

Michael grinned. "I hope you're right, Mama. Lady would be ashamed to have a little Yankee sissy for a son." Lady nickered as if in agreement. Dixie giggled.

Papa frowned. "You'd better mind your tongue, Michael. Just because they are our oppressors doesn't make the Yankees sissies."

"I'm sorry, Papa."

"Besides," Papa continued, "Do you think your cousins Philip, Allen, Drew and Charles are sissies?"

Michael shook his head. "No."

"I'm sure the other side of the family is proud of them for joining the Union," Papa said.

"I'm sure they are. But I must admit, I don't like them quite as much as I used to. I do wish the Yanks would get off their high horse though."

"Michael," Papa said, "I know what you're trying to say, but you should find another way to put it."

"Yes, sir."

Michael and Dixie soon left to finish building a hay fort in the barn. The Nace children were coming over and the fort was to be their hide out.

Ellen was lost in thought. Silas stood in front of her. "Where are your thoughts transporting you to? Are you still here or somewhere in Virginia?" he teased.

She shook her head as if to clear her mind and smiled. A gentle breeze tousled Silas's reddish brown hair and blew sprigs of Ellen's dark blonde hair into her face. She pushed it back behind her ear.

"I'm here because you and two of my children are here. But, I'm in Virginia too, because my two oldest are there." Silas nodded understandingly.

Ellen sighed. "I'm concerned for them, Silas. I'm concerned about Richard and Seth being out there away from us. They're still young. I'm sure they feel pretty grown up, but they are still just children."

Silas placed an arm around her shoulder. "When your country calls, dear, age doesn't matter."

Ellen looked up at him with concern. Was he considering himself "called by his country"? But his next words put her at ease. "Sometimes she calls you to service, sometimes to remain on the home front, but we are all defenders. Young or old, we all have to do our duty for our country."

"I know what you mean…" she looked over towards the barn just as the loft window swung open. Michael's head popped out and upon seeing his parents, he waved. They waved back.

Turning back to their conversation, Ellen said, "Silas, I'm also worried about Michael. He seems to be developing a bad attitude toward the Northern people."

Silas resisted the impulse to smile. "You're right, dear. I suppose we haven't exactly helped there. We've always talked about the Yanks in a negative light in front of him." Ellen flinched a little at the reference to northerners as Yanks. Silas noticed and tried even harder to hide his smile.

He continued, "We need to help Michael understand it isn't the people we are against, but rather their views. I don't want him to hate the people. That's the worst thing that he could do."

"I agree. I don't think he even realizes that he's leaving himself open for hatred to grow in his heart," Ellen said.

"I'll have a talk with him soon. He doesn't hate them yet, and I don't want that to happen."

Ellen nodded gratefully. The smile finally made its way to Silas' mouth. "Does the term Yankees bother you, dear?"

She just looked at him as a snicker escaped his lips. "I'm sorry, Ellen."

A smile slowly spread across her face. "It's alright," she said, laughing softly.

Her eyes once again took on that far off look and the smile disappeared. "I wonder how that battle turned out yesterday. I hope and pray the boys came through okay." Ellen's voice shook as she spoke for fear her sons had been hurt or…She shook her head. She couldn't dwell on these things. She had to trust God.

★ 1861 ★

Chapter 12
★

"It Never Gets Easier"

We then that are strong ought to bear the infirmities of the weak, and
not to please ourselves.
Romans 15:1

"...We had to keep and to care for, more than five hundred bruised
bodies of men, men made in the image of God, marred by the hand of
men..."
Joshua L. Chamberlain

S eth had a new assignment, assisting a surgeon. There was
plenty of work to be done and not enough people to do it.
Seth was eager to help. Maybe he could be a doctor someday
after all!

He started the Wednesday after the battle, and as long as
he lived, Seth would remember his very first experience with
amputations...

Seth quickly went in search of the surgeon. The sun was
hot, making the wounded even more miserable. Seth passed tent
after tent of wounded soldiers.

One, who looked a little older than Michael, lay in his
tent writhing in pain. Seth watched as he was carefully carried

into a nearby tent, which Seth realized was the surgeon's tent. The surgeon stepped out of the tent and motioned Seth over to him.

"You're that Mason boy, right?"

"Yes, sir."

"What's your first name?"

"Seth."

"Well, Seth, I've got your first job ready. I have to take this boy's leg off," he said pointing toward the tent. "I need you to help keep him still. Think you can handle that?"

"I believe I can," Seth said, somewhat nervously.

The kind doctor smiled. "I think you'll do fine. By the way, you can call me Dr. Jennings." Seth sat down on a barrel next to the "operating table" with his back to the young boy's leg, which was badly infected. It should have been treated the day of the battle, but due to the shortage of doctors, it had not been properly cared for.

A few tears trickled down the feverish boy's face. The doctor left to find Chaplain Eric Davis, an older grandfatherly man. The boy turned his head to look at Seth. "Why? Why do they have to take my leg?" he asked, though with much effort. His breathing was labored.

Seth thought the answer was rather obvious, but he also knew that, although the boy wasn't delirious, the fever might have him somewhat disoriented. Before Seth could answer him, Dr. Jennings's aide said rather harshly, "Because there's nothing else that can be done."

"Why don't we try to think about something else?" Seth suggested. "Where are you from?"

"Richmond. Well, two miles out of the city limits."

"Interesting. I'm from Four Tree Springs, North Carolina. Oh, my name's Seth Mason."

"My name's Nate Bowers." The boy jerked in pain. He squeezed Seth's arm tightly. Just then, Chaplain Davis stepped in with a sorrowful expression on his face. He stepped up to the "table" and laid his hand gently on Nate's shoulder.

"Nate, I'm sorry this has happened to you. We may not understand it now, but someday, maybe in heaven we'll understand the reason. May I pray with you, son?"

"Yes, please," said Nate weakly. Seth bowed his head as the chaplain knelt down and began to pray.

"Dear Father, we've come before You to pray for Nate Bowers. Lord, we pray that You will protect him during the surgery and that You will guide the doctor's hands as he performs the surgery." Here, Chaplain Davis cleared his throat. He reached over and gripped Nate's hand tightly as he continued.

"We ask Thy blessings upon Nate, Lord. Please ward off any diseases that may try to attack his poor body. Please strengthen him, both physically and spiritually. We will thank You and do thank You for what You're gonna do. We ask these things in the Name of Jesus, Amen."

"Amen," responded the others. The chaplain left and the doctor's aide gave Nate some medicine that Seth had never heard of. It was supposed to ease the pain.

"You will feel some pain," the doctor said as he reached for his knife, "but not as much as you would without the medicine."

After waiting a few minutes for the medicine to take effect, Dr. Jennings began. Nate closed his eyes and squeezed Seth's arm tighter.

Except for a few grunts and moans, Nate remained relatively calm…until the doctor reached the bone. Nate gave an involuntary scream. Immediately Seth and the aide took hold of Nate's shoulders to keep him still as Dr. Jennings continued to work.

"You're doing fine, Nate," Seth whispered in his ear. "It'll all be over soon."

Dr. Jennings finished up quickly, bandaged the wound and then it was all over. Nate was drawn up in pain. "If that medicine reduced the pain, I can't imagine what it would have been like *without* the medicine!" Nate said, still trying to catch his breath. He was pale and sweat was dripping off his forehead.

Dr. Jennings patted him on the shoulder. "It's over now. That's probably the worst pain you'll ever go through."

Nate gripped Seth's arm once more as another spasm of pain hit him. "Just breathe through it, Nate. It's alright now." The boy began to relax and wearily closed his eyes.

When Dr. Jennings gave his approval, Seth carried Nate back to his tent. The doctor's aide followed with some more medicine. Once Seth had Nate situated on his cot, the aide took over and told Seth to go on back, much to Nate's displeasure. Seth promised Nate he would come back later. He returned to the surgeon's tent.

Dr. Jennings looked up. "It never gets easier, Seth. I feel like a villain, even though that surgery might very well save his life. What does he have to look forward to now? A life of being an invalid, that's what! Makes me want to go and drag that Lincoln fellow right out of the White House and let him see what his men did to the boy. That boy wouldn't have been out there if Lincoln had just left well enough alone! He'd be safe at home with his mama. I wish I could get my hands on the Yankee that shot the cannon that did the damage!"

Seth looked down. His parents had told him never to say anything disrespectful about Mr. Lincoln. He was a man in authority, even though they knew he was wrong.

Seth wondered what his father would say if he could see Nate and the other soldiers. Would he still think Mr. Lincoln should be respected? Seth knew his father would be upset, but he wouldn't say *everything* he thought. Neither would Mama.

"Seth, what do you think about him?" Seth quickly came back to reality.

"Pardon?"

"What do you think about that Lincoln fellow?"

"Well, I think he might see things differently if he did see the results of his decision. I can't say exactly what I think about him, because I don't think it would be respectful. I've been praying that God would touch his heart and let him see his mistake before more lives are lost."

Dr. Jennings stared at Seth for a moment. "Son, you put me to shame. Here I am ranting and raving about the man real hateful like, and you stand there and say you're praying for him. Your parents raised you well. You stick right to that way of thinking."

They treated a number of soldiers that day, but Seth couldn't bring himself to watch the amputations yet. It wasn't the blood that bothered him, just the idea of cutting off a part of a human being.

In between patients Dr. Jennings talked to Seth about his desire to be a doctor. He was very encouraging to the young man and offered to teach him some "arts of the trade." Seth was elated. Free training! God's ways are always best.

★ 1861 ★

Seth found Richard and Tyler soon after Dr. Jennings dismissed him for a short break. They were sitting under a tree talking when Seth walked up. Richard looked up as Seth sat down next to Tyler. "Hey, leaving your post already?" Richard teased.

Seth grinned at his brother. "Just taking a break."

Tyler nodded. "We just now got a chance to sit down. How's your new job going?"

Seth gave his friend a half smile. "As well as it can." Tyler noticed something was wrong. Seth was usually pretty perky. Now he was dismal.

"What's eating at you, Seth?" Richard asked quizzically. A sigh escaped Seth's lips. He told the boys about Nate Bowers and the amputation and about the indifferent doctor's aide.

The boys sat in silence after hearing about Nate. Richard shook his head. He was glad Michael was safe at home with his Papa and Mama.

"But on a happier note, Dr. Jennings has offered to teach me more about doctoring. He says if I work hard, I may be a doctor sooner than I planned!"

The break ended all too soon, and the boys got back to their camp duties, such as hauling water and chopping wood, or in Seth's case, tending more wounded.

Later, after joining Richard, Jordan and Tyler for supper, Seth went to see Nate. He was about to enter the tent, when a shout from behind stopped him. Turning around, Seth saw the doctor's aide coming toward him. "Mason, Seth Mason, right?"

"Yes, sir."

"I'd like you to stay away from Nate." These words surprised Seth. He hadn't expected him to say that.

"May I ask why?" he asked, a little agitated.

The aide replied, "Nothing personal, it's just that Nate doesn't need any visitors right now. He needs plenty of rest. Another time would be better."

Before Seth could say anything, a weak voice came from inside the tent. "David, I want to see him. Let him in."

"No, Nate, you need to rest. Visitors will make you tired and ruin your health."

Seth raised one eyebrow, knowing David was exaggerating the matter. Nate wasn't through arguing his plea yet.

"David, let me see him or I won't be able to rest at all. I need to talk to him." The two disputed for a few minutes while Seth stood there, unsure of what to do. Nate finally won out, and Seth was allowed into the tent. David walked away, albeit upset, but he said nothing.

"Please excuse David," Nate said as Seth took a seat next to him. "He ain't mad at you. He just doesn't want me to overdo it. You might know by now that David is my brother."

This might have surprised Seth had it not been for their dispute. Patients didn't usually call doctors or aides by their first name.

"The reason I asked you to come back by here," Nate continued, "was because, first of all, I wanted to thank you for being there for me when I had my amputation. You didn't even know me, yet you stayed there by me. I really needed you. I'm sure you would rather have done anything else than assist in an amputation."

Seth looked down, then back up at Nate. "I only did what I would have wanted someone to do for me. It's my job. I didn't do anything great."

"Well, it was something great for me," Nate said earnestly. "Secondly, I wanted to ask you, are you a follower of Jesus?"

Seth grinned. "Yes, I am. I've been a child of the Savior for about eleven years now. In fact, my spiritual birthday was the same day as the battle."

"Oh! What a way to celebrate!" They both laughed. Seth then looked Nate in the eye.

"Nate, are *you* a child of God?" Nate smiled.

"Yes. I actually submitted to Him two years ago. Now I'm working on my brother. He needs Jesus in his life so bad. I think he's angry at God for taking our Papa home to heaven two years ago. Our Mama remarried right before the war began. I call him 'Papa Joe, but David calls him, 'Mr. Fane.' That's his last name. He won't accept him and move on with life. I don't understand why God took Papa, but now, I understand better what my Mama means by, 'The Lord giveth and the Lord taketh away. Blessed be the name of the Lord.'"

"Amen. I'm sorry about your Papa, but your Mama's right. You just trust the Lord and do what's right. I'll pray for your brother right now if you want."

"Yes, please do that!" So the two prayed, pleading with the Lord for David's salvation.

★1861★

Silas glanced up from his newspaper. Ellen was pacing the floor in his office. "Ellen, Michael will be back with the mail soon. But, dear, please don't get your hopes up. The mail does travel awful slow."

Ellen turned towards her husband. "It's been four days since the battle and we haven't heard a word about the boys. Oh, Silas! What if no word is coming at all?"

"Don't even think like that!" Silas said, a little sharper than he intended to. Recovering, he added quickly, "We can't allow ourselves to imagine the worst when there is no cause for it."

Just as Silas predicted, there was no word from the boys. Ellen felt sick. What had happened to her boys? Where were they? Had they been hurt in anyway? She thought of how young Seth was. Too young to see the scenes of war, she told herself. Why had they let him go? And Richard should be at home right this minute helping Silas manage Shady Grove.

Dixie too was struggling, missing her brothers immensely. More than once she had locked herself into her room to pray and cry.

The men folk handled their worry in secret and certainly more composedly than the ladies, but they were just as concerned for the two missing family members.

Saturday rolled around and still no word. It was torture to the anxious family. What had become of Richard and Seth?

★ 1861 ★

Chapter 13

★

Eternity

For after that in the wisdom of God the world by wisdom knew not
God, it pleased God by the foolishness of preaching to save them
that believe.
I Corinthians 1:21

Because it took time to get all the wounded transferred from the field to hospitals, a few of Jackson's men had been assigned to help with the wounded. Among them were Richard, Seth, Tyler, Jordan and Titus Mallory.

The field hospital had moved a few miles from the original battle site and was running a little more efficiently, but they were still under staffed.

It was strange not being with their brigade, but that didn't mean they weren't drilling. Oh no. They drilled in the morning, did chores, and drilled again in the evening.

But at the moment Seth is awaiting an explanation from David Bowers. "David, this is ridiculous! Every time I try to visit Nate, you try to run me off! Why won't you let me in? I promised-"

"I don't care what you promised. I have my reasons and I don't have to explain them to you. Now get out of here," David replied coldly. "Besides," he continued sneeringly, "I've had enough of your religious conversations, preacher boy." Seth's countenance fell. So that was the reason for the daily struggle to gain access to Nate.

"David, Nate has asked me to talk with him about spiritual things. The chaplain can't be with every soldier all the time, so Nate asks me the questions that are on his mind. We discuss Biblical truths that will help him grow spiritually. We want to live it the way the Bible tells us to, not say we believe it and then not live it. David, please let me in."

David's face reflected his skepticism. Seth's light blue eyes were pleading, and his gaze was unwavering. David swallowed, feeling himself beginning to back down.

Unbeknownst to the boys, Chaplain Davis had observed the whole situation. Nate had told him about David's trying to keep Seth away from him. He wasn't at all pleased with the older brother's actions, and the chaplain decided to take action.

"David." Both boys were startled by Chaplain Davis' deep voice. "Let Seth see Nate. He hasn't done anything wrong. Besides, I need to talk to you." David stepped out of Seth's way, and Seth entered the tent. Chaplain Davis motioned for David to come with him and the two soon walked away.

Seth sat down next to Nate's pallet and waited for Nate to acknowledge his presence. The young boy painfully rolled over to look at his visitor. Nate's eyes were dull, his breathing slow, but his countenance was cheery and peaceful.

"Hey...Seth. Glad you...came. I need to...to tell you...something." He struggled to get a deep breath. It pained Seth to see his younger friend suffer, but some people got worse before they got better. This was of very little comfort.

Seth winced as he heard the familiar rattle when Nate took a breath. *Please, Lord, don't let him have pneumonia! Please, no!* But Seth knew it was true. Nate had the tell-tale signs.

"Seth, Dr. Jennings told me this morning that I probably won't live much longer." Nate spoke slowly and softly, as if it took all his strength to get the words out.

NO! Seth couldn't stand the thought of losing his friend. *Dear Lord, please, no!* Much to his surprise, Nate began to console him.

"Seth, don't be sad. Be happy for me. I'll see you again someday in heaven. God has given me peace about dying. I don't have to worry about it. Seth, can't you see? I'll see Jesus and my Papa. I'll never hurt again. I'm so excited, I just can't wait to get there."

Seth buried his face in his hands. He'd only known Nate for a few days, and now he was dying. It didn't seem right…Nate was so young!

They talked a bit longer, and then Seth left to let Nate rest. He hurried away, thinking over his conversation with Nate. He had to get back to work in five minutes, so taking a deep breath, he walked calmly toward Dr. Jennings' tent.

★1861★

Michael ran as fast as his legs could carry him. "PAPA! MAMA! A letter! From Richard and Seth!"

It was Monday, over a week since the battle. The family gathered in the front yard as Michael handed the letter to Papa. Silas's fingers seemed all thumbs as he tried to open the letter. At last he managed to open it and read aloud:

Dear Family,

I hope this letter reached you with all speed. We are alright. Let me repeat it; we came through the battle with nary a scratch and are ALRIGHT. Mama may need to hear this more than once! And as I know you are curious, I am glad to tell you that we won the battle, thank the Lord!

I am writing this just after the battle. It is late. I'm afraid this note must be kept short, but I will share a need with you. We need more doctors and nurses here. Any and all

*help would be welcomed as we are very understaffed. We
need your prayers. There are many hundreds wounded.*

Will write in more detail after things have calmed down.

We Love and Miss Y'all!
Richard and Seth

Ellen cried tears of relief. Her boys were safe. They had
survived their first battle. And at last, she could relax. She
thought of the boys' prayer request. More help needed? She
looked at her husband and their eyes met.

A smiled played at Silas' lips. He whispered to her,
"Let's pray first, then talk to Pastor Brewster."

★ 1861 ★

David and Chaplain Davis entered the chaplain's tent.
After being seated, the preacher spoke what was on his heart.
"David, I've come to realize that there's a problem between you
and the Mason boy. Why is that?"

David scowled. "I don't like Seth's preaching. I stay
with Nate most of the time. Especially since…" He looked
down.

"Ever since the amputation?" the chaplain finished.

David nodded. "Because of that, I have to listen to Nate
tell me about all of his and Seth's religious conversations. I'm
sick of it. I can't get a good night's sleep because of it. I'm really
tired of it!"

Chaplain Davis nodded thoughtfully. David felt his face
turning red. Imagine, saying things like that to a chaplain! What
was he thinking? Complaining about the very thing this man
promotes! Why, oh, why hadn't he thought before he spoke?
The more David thought about it, the more agitated he became.

"David," the chaplain began, "Seth's just trying to help
Nate get through a difficult time of his life. He's not trying to
hurt you in any way. And Nate? Well, naturally, since you're his

115

brother, he wants to tell you about the things that are important to him. It's helping him and, dare I say, he wants it to help you through this trial as well. True, you haven't lost a leg, but you have to watch Nate suffering through this. He wants you to have the peace he has through it all."

David turned his face away. He couldn't help but think of the preacher who had come to the house when his father had passed away two years ago. That man had tried to help his family too. He was kind, grandfatherly…and truly wanted to comfort them. In fact he was the one who led Nate to the Lord.

But David had not been one to be comforted. He had ignored the man and walked away. "I don't need anything from anyone," he had told the preacher. "I just need to be alone."

Part of him wanted to do the same to this preacher, just walk away and stop his ears to the counsel he offered. But something else seemed to compel him to stay…was it the kindness in his eyes? His gentle manner? His sincerity? Something about this chaplain seemed to hold David captive to every word he spoke.

Chaplain Davis looked David in the eye and brought him back from his thoughts. "How *is* Nate doing?"

"He's gonna die," David said bluntly.

"Have you sent word to your mother?"

David closed his eyes. *Mama,* he thought. *This will kill her!* "No, not yet. I don't know how to tell her."

"David," asked the chaplain slowly, "Is your mother a believer?"

David just nodded. Chaplain Davis continued, "Has she ever tried to share the gospel with you?"

David looked away once more. *Why did he have to ask that?* Chaplain Davis could tell that he was on the right track. Finally David responded, "Yes, she has."

"Then she too wishes to see you at peace with God. David, losing Nate will be hard for your mother, but she will see him again. But what if it was you laying there dying? Losing you would be harder, David, since you haven't accepted Christ as your Savior. She would never see you again. And you would never see her again."

David looked up at that last sentence. He'd never really considered that. He opened his mouth to say something, but couldn't get the words to form. Never see her again? The very thought made all the color drain from his face. David Bowers may have been a stern young man, but he loved his mother more than anyone else in the world. He didn't like the idea of never seeing her again at all.

"I...I don't want that to happen," he stammered.

Chaplain Davis placed a hand on David's shoulder. "I know you don't, but what's worse than that, David, is that you will forever be separated from God. There is no hope for you after death. And let's be honest, since this war has begun, we've all thought about death. In the book of James, the Bible tells us our life is, '...*a vapor, that appeareth for a little time, and then vanisheth away*.'"

David sighed. That was the very reason he hadn't been sleeping well for the last few days. "I try not to think about dying. It's too uncertain."

"David, don't push away your questions and fears."

David shrugged. "Sometimes it's better than facing them."

"Is that why you don't want Seth visiting Nate?"

"Seth and Nate keep preaching at me. I've got to deal with it somehow, so I've eliminated part of the problem. But I can deal with Nate."

Chaplain Davis reached for his Bible. "Son, may I share some scriptures with you? I'd like to show you a few things that will help you."

"Might as well," David consented. He'd heard the stuff before. What harm could it do?

Chaplain Davis thumbed through the well-worn copy of God's Word. He turned to Isaiah 57:20. "You mentioned you aren't getting any sleep at night. Did you know your situation is mentioned in the Bible? It says here, '*But the wicked are like the troubled sea, when it cannot rest, whose waters cast up mire and*

117

dirt.' You won't be able to rest until you submit your life to God, David. He is the only one who can give you rest. The next verse says, *'There is no peace, saith my God, to the wicked.'"*

David stared hard at the Bible in Chaplain Davis' hands. *He's right,* David thought. *I can't rest and I have no peace of mind. And I'm definitely one of the wicked he's talking about.*

The chaplain continued. "All of us are sinners, David. Because of Adam's sin in the garden, we are all born sinners. Romans 3:10 says, *'As it is written, There is none righteous, no, not one:'* And because of this sinful nature of ours, we are all doomed for a place called hell. I know you've heard of hell before, but really think about it. The Bible says it's a place of fire and brimstone. You're constantly in pain, on fire, and in outer darkness."

Perspiration glistened on David's forehead. *This man is convincing,* he thought. *The way he describes it, his tone and countenance...it's like he knows this place is real.*

"God does have an alternative though," the chaplain said, excitement in his voice. "Heaven is for the followers of Christ. No sin can enter there. But there is no way we can get rid of our sin by our own efforts. So God sent His Son Jesus to earth to die on the cross for us. He took every sin ever committed and that ever will be committed upon Himself and died for them. Jesus was perfect and only perfection can pay the sin penalty. He laid down His Life for us. He was dead and buried but arose three days later. He did all that so that we could live with Him in heaven someday if we will only ask His forgiveness and ask Him to save us. David, has there ever been a time in your life when you asked Jesus to save you?"

Bitterness swept through David's heart. "No, I never have. I know Nate has. But what good has it done him? He said the prayer and look at him now! He's dying. Why would God let that happen to one who believed in Him?"

Chaplain Davis silently prayed for help. "Being a Christian doesn't mean bad things won't happen to you. It means you have someone to turn to for strength when the trials come. You don't have to face them alone; Jesus cares about you and can give you peace."

"Then how do you get that peace?" David asked skeptically.

" *'Believe on the Lord Jesus Christ and thou shalt be saved',*" Chaplain Davis replied. "Believe that He died on the cross, was buried and rose again on the third day and that He is able to save you. Pray and ask Him to take away your sins, and you're guaranteed a home in Heaven. Just put yourself into God's hands, trust Him as your Savior, and you will have nothing to fear. You have nothing to lose and all to gain. David, do you believe this?"

David's head was bowed. He was silent for a moment. Then he began to speak. "I do believe it, and I really do want what Nate's got." He stopped and cleared his throat. David was not one to easily show his emotions, and he wasn't wanting to now. But the Holy Spirit was really working on him.

"Wouldn't you like to take care of this right now, David?"

A battle was raging within him. *I've needed to do this for a long time,* David thought. *But I just don't know…I'm tired of running from it, but I'll have to give up so much…* He wiped sweat off his forehead. *Why is it so hard to make up my mind? Like the chaplain said, I have nothing to lose and all to gain…Separated from God and Mama forever? No. I can't let that happen. But maybe another time…*

David didn't speak for a few moments, but when he did, his decision was made. "Yes, I want to settle it right here, right now. I'm tired of running. And I don't want to spend eternity in hell, away from God…or my family. I've known I needed to do this for years, but I'm done fighting. I need God in my life."

"Thank the Lord! David, let's kneel right here and you just ask Jesus to forgive you."

They both knelt by the chaplain's cot, and David began to pray. When David stood up, he was a different man.

Chaplain Davis gave David a hardy embrace and nearly shouted, "Praise the Lord! There is joy in the presence of the angels today, David! Oh, Praise God's Holy Name!"

David shook the chaplain's hand. "Thank you for your help. But if you'll excuse me, I need to go see my brother."

 ★ 1861 ★

Chapter 14
★
Surprised

Come now, and let us reason together, saith the LORD: though your
sins be as scarlet, they shall be as white as snow...
Isaiah 1:18a

David listened outside of Nate's tent before entering. *Good,*
he thought, *Seth's already left.* He pulled open the tent flap
and stepped inside. "You awake, Nate?"

"Yep," came a muffled reply as Nate rolled onto his
back. He looked up at his brother. David's eyes were shining
with excitement. "What's happened? You look like you just
whipped a Yankee regiment single-handedly. What is it?"

David grinned and sat down next to his brother. "Nate,
I've made an important decision and you need to know about
it."

Uh-oh, Nate thought, *maybe he's decided not to let Seth*
come back here at all! No, David looks too happy. What could
he be up to?

"Nate, I've needed to do this for a long time, and today,
I gave my life to Christ. I belong to Him now, so you can stop
worrying about me."

"Oh, Praise the Lord!" Nate tried to sit up to hug his brother, but David met him halfway. Nate, despite his weakening condition, hugged his brother tightly. A few tears of joy and relief trickled down the boy's face. His brother was saved at last.

Nate wiped his eyes. "Mama will be so happy, David! You have to write her!"

David nodded in agreement. "I'm going to. I won't get a chance today, but I'll write her soon. Nate, do you want me to tell her about you too?"

The younger boy was silent for a minute. "No, I'd like to tell her. It might be easier for her to hear it from me."

"Alright. After I've written mine, I'll help you write yours."

Nate nodded slowly. "I wish she didn't have to know. It's gonna be hard for her." He sighed. "I should have been more careful during the fight. I should have paid more attention."

"Nate, it's not your fault. You were hit by cannon fragments, and there wasn't anything you could have done about that. I guess God's got a reason for this too. Christianity is a new thing for me, but Mama always quoted a verse about all things working together for good to those who love God. I guess that would apply to us."

Nate nodded. "You're right."

David smiled. "Well, I need to get back to work. Pray for me; I need to talk to Seth, and I'm not sure what to say yet."

A wide grin was on Nate's face. "If I see him, I'll tell him you're looking for him."

★ 1861 ★

Seth grunted as he leaned all his weight down on a crowbar, trying to open a crate of supplies. The lid flew off and Seth nearly lost his balance but smiled with satisfaction. At least the lid hadn't hit Dr. Jennings.

He removed a small box of bandages from the crate and handed it to the doctor who opened the box and used the bandages on his most recent patient.

David hurried into the tent. Dr. Jennings frowned. "You've been gone a long time. What kept you?"

"I was talking to Chaplain Davis, then I needed to tell Nate something. I'm sorry I'm late, Dr. Jennings."

The doctor had been irritated, but upon hearing that David had been talking to the chaplain, his tone changed. "That's fine, David. Give Seth a hand taking this fella back to his tent," he said, motioning to the soldier lying on the table. "Seth knows where it is."

"Yes, sir."

Silence reigned as they helped the sick man to his tent, but when they were making the return trip, David broke the stillness. "Seth, I...I feel like I owe you an apology."

Seth glanced at David in surprise. "Oh?"

"I'm sorry I've been running you off when you tried to talk with Nate. And I'm sorry for my words. I had a talk with the chaplain today. I've settled some things in my heart. I'm walking in the same direction as you and Nate now. I wanted you to know and I would like to ask your forgiveness for my past actions."

Seth's expressions had changed several times during this speech. Surprise, shock, and joy had taken turns on his face. He grinned broadly and extended his hand to his new brother in Christ. "Of course I forgive you! David, this is wonderful! Praise God! And you've told Nate?"

"Yes. I told him first. Seth, I wish I'd done this long ago. I needed this when my father passed away, but I was too stubborn."

Seth placed a hand on David's shoulder. "The important thing is that you're saved now. You can't change the past. Learn from it, and press on with your new life in Christ."

David smiled. "Thanks, Seth. I needed to hear that."

 ★1861★

"Pvt. Mason, you're ordered to go to the train station to collect donations for the medical camp and escort some volunteers to camp."

"Yes, sir."

Richard hitched Champion up to an ambulance wagon and headed for the depot. It was hard to believe the battle had taken place nearly two weeks ago! He scanned the depot platform for the crates listed on the receipt he held in his hand.

"Richard!" He turned and couldn't believe his eyes. There was Dixie, hurrying towards him. He ran to his sister. Meeting her half way, he picked her up in his excitement. He swung her around, hugging her tightly. She returned his embrace warmly.

He kissed her forehead and set her down, still hugging her. "How did you get here? Who's with you? How is everybody back home? Oh, Mama, you're here too!" Richard said, releasing Dixie and hugging his mother. Richard's questions kept tumbling out.

At last he stopped to get some of his answers. "We prayed about the help for the camp," Mama began. "And God laid it on our hearts for us to come. Lana came with us and Isaac was our escort, since his marching orders sent him up here anyway."

It wasn't until then that Richard caught sight of Isaac and Lana. He exchanged greetings with them. Richard was still grinning excitedly. "Let's get y'all and the donations to the camp. Seth will be glad to see y'all! He'll be with Dr. Jennings. Come on, he should be finishing his shift soon."

Meanwhile at the surgeon's tent, Seth took a wet rag and rubbed blood off his hands from their last patient. Dr. Jennings looked up from his own cleaning and saw Richard and the others standing outside. Richard pointed to Seth, then to his mother.

The doctor grinned and turned towards Seth. "David said that was the last man for today. You can go on now. I'll finish up here."

Seth nodded. "Thank you, sir. I'll be back here after drill tomorrow."

"Good."

Seth grabbed his hat from a nearby table and placed it on his head. He stepped outside. His eyes locked with his mother's. A look of shock crossed his face. "Mama!" Seth was soon hugging her. Eventually, he saw his sister and the others and greeted them. Like Richard he was full of questions.

Richard suggested they go back to their campsite and talk there. Soon everyone had gathered around the fire pit and lively conversation followed. When things were calmer and Dixie got a chance, she told Seth about the colts.

"They're so cute! I can't wait 'till you can see them. Confederate plays with them as if he were a baby again." They all laughed.

Meanwhile, Tyler was delivering letters around the camp. He only had two left; one for Alvin Willis and another for Jeremy Calling.

Looking up, he saw Lana sitting around the campfire with the others. In his excitement at seeing his cousin, he handed Jeremy Alvin's letter and Alvin Jeremy's letter. The two looked quizzically at each other as they switched letters.

"Wonder what's eating at him," Alvin said aloud.

Jeremy looked over at Alvin. "What?"

"I said, I wonder what's eating at him."

"I don't think I've ever heard that expression before," Jeremy said, laughing a little.

Alvin looked surprised. "Oh, it just means 'what's on his mind?' You reckon he knows them people over there with Richard and Seth?"

"Maybe," Jeremy said, slitting open his own letter, "Hey, it's from my Grandma Calling!" Alvin shrugged and opened his letter from his sister.

Tyler hurried over to join the group at the fire pit. He sat down next to Lana, who gave her younger cousin a side hug. As Lana began answering his questions about why they were there, another voice joined the group. "Y'all are having a party and didn't invite me?"

Dixie grinned as her cousin Jordan sat down across from her. After another round of explanations, everyone resumed their conversations. Dixie moved over next to her cousin. "Alexandria and Cynthia said to tell you they miss you and want to see you really bad," she said. "Cindy even said she wished she was allowed to come with us to help in the camp."

Jordan laughed at the idea of his little sister, just five years old, coming and bandaging heads and cleaning wounds. "She's a sweetheart. Who knows? Maybe she would have been a morale booster to the wounded if she had come!"

Dixie laughed. "Maybe next time," she teased. "Alexandria really wants a letter from you for her birthday. Aunt Marianna told me she had mentioned it and asked if I could pass the word along."

Jordan nodded. "She'll get it. I'll send it back with y'all. It's hard to believe she'll be ten! The girls are growing up so fast!"

Ellen nodded at her nephew's comment. "Children have a way of doing that. Richard's still supposed to be in school in my mind's eye and Michael's still just a baby."

Richard placed his arm around his mother. "If it'll make you feel better, Mama, I'll go back to school when we get home," he joked.

Mama just smiled and returned the hug. The conversation soon drifted to a sermon the boys had heard the day before on spiritual warfare. "It was really good," Tyler said earnestly. "I learned a lot from it."

Lana smiled at her cousin. He seemed so relaxed and peaceful. Something had changed about him. He no longer bore that troubled look that had clouded his face the last few months. *Perhaps at last, he has settled with God whatever it was that was bothering him,* Lana thought.

"I didn't know you had company today, Mason." The group turned toward Titus Mallory who was addressing Richard.

Richard stood and shook hands with his friend. "I didn't either 'til about an hour ago. Titus, I'd like to introduce you to my Mother, my sister, Dixianna, our pastor's daughter, Miss Lana Brewster, and my cousin, Isaac Mason." Turning to his family he said, "This is Cpl. Titus Mallory, V.M.I cadet."

Titus laughed at his introduction. "Former V.M.I. cadet. I've traded that in for a position in the Confederate army." Handshakes were exchanged and Titus joined their conversation.

Tyler glanced at the pocket watch in his hand, and whistled in surprise. "It's nearly curfew time! We need to get the ladies to the boarding house and get back to camp, pronto!"

"Alright, let's go!" Richard declared as the group stood to leave.

Titus took off his hat. "It was a pleasure to meet you, ladies and you too, Isaac," he said, shaking hands with Isaac. He gave a bow as they prepared to go.

"Likewise, Cpl. Mallory," Mama said as she returned his bow with a curtsy. The girls followed her example.

Seth, Tyler and Richard escorted the ladies to the boarding house. The boys brought their lightweight trunks into the room.

Mama, Lana and Dixie bid the men good night and farewell, then readied for bed. As they drifted off to sleep, they knew tomorrow would be a busy day.

★1861★

Chapter 15
★
More Than One Way to Serve

And of some have compassion, making a difference:
Jude 22
◇◇★◇◇
"I have never worked so hard in my life and I would rather do that
than anything else in the world."
Susan Lee Blackford (Confederate Nurse)

Michael was bored. With Dixie and Mama gone there was nothing, he thought, exciting to do. The farm work was done, and Papa had paperwork to do. Finally, he decided to see if he could go over to the Naces' and go fishing with Carter.

Papa had no objections, but there was a stipulation: he had to take some sewing notions to Mrs. Nace. His mother had promised them to her, and Papa kept forgetting to give them to her husband.

Michael carried the basket of notions, his pole and a bucket of worms down the half mile road to the Naces' farm. As he turned into the Nace's yard, Annie Nace came out and invited Michael inside. Michael explained his deliveries, and Annie motioned for him to follow her.

He set his fishing pole down on the porch and carried the basket inside. As they entered the kitchen, Michael saw Jonathan and Kathie Nace sitting at the table with Alyssa Rose. Mr. Nace smiled. "Hey, Michael, how are you?"

"I'm fine. How are y'all?"

"Good, thank you."

"Are we interrupting anything, Mama?" asked Annie.

"Oh no, we're finished. Michael, are you alone today?"

"Yes, ma'am. Here's that sewing stuff Mama said she'd give y'all. I was going to see if Carter could go fishing today."

At that moment Carter bounded into the kitchen. "Michael! There you are! It's great to see you! I just came from your place to see if you could go fishing, but your Papa said you had come over here. Widow Lanier invited me to fish in her pond and told me to ask you to come too. How about it?"

"Sure, that's one of the reasons I came over, to ask you to go fishing. The fish have been biting like crazy."

"Let's go!" Carter said, eager to be off. Mr. and Mrs. Nace laughed.

"You boys have fun!" said Mrs. Nace. "Don't get into trouble!" she teased.

★ 1861 ★

"Attention!" The soldiers stood super straight. It was drill time and no one wanted to do extra drills in the scorching sun. "Right face!" They all turned to the right. Seth was gripping his rifle so tightly, his knuckles were turning white.

"Relax, Mason. Don't lock your knees," instructed Alvin, who was standing behind him. Seth nodded. His nervousness lessened a little, but not much. The colonel's wife, son-in-law and daughter were visiting the camp and had decided to watch.

This was only part of the cause for Seth's nervousness. He'd messed up terribly in their last drill, and he was afraid of messing up again. A few of the soldiers had grumbled about him making drill take longer in the hot sun.

129

A drummer was standing next to Seth and didn't appear the least bit nervous. "Shoulder arms!" Seth lifted his rifle up and carefully shouldered it. "Forward, March!" The drummer boys began the steady beat and the column of soldiers started forward. After the march they were brought to a halt back at their original position.

"About face!" The sergeant began inspecting their rifles next. The sergeant usually did this first, but today, he'd decided to throw off the routine a little. Seth relaxed as he remembered that he'd cleaned his rifle early that morning.

About that time Seth started feeling lightheaded. Everything started to spin. The last thing Seth remembered before falling flat on his back was the colonel's wife saying, "He's falling!"

"...must have locked his knees," Seth heard someone say, though they sounded muffled to him. He shook his head groggily. Seth tried to sit up, but fell back unconscious from getting up too fast. A few moments later he woke up to the colonel's wife dabbing a cool cloth on his head. A dozen faces bobbed around in Seth's blurred vision. He tried once again to get up, but the colonel had two soldiers hold him down.

"Seth, don't try to sit up. Just rest a minute. It's alright Seth, relax." Seth looked up at Richard, who was kneeling in front of him. Seth felt dizzy and closed his eyes.

"Sergeant, have two of your men take him to his tent. Let him rest a little," the colonel ordered.

"Yes, sir! Mason, Nace, take him to his quarters."

"Yes, sir!" they said in unison. They helped Seth slowly to his feet and then left for the tents.

The colonel's wife followed, carrying on as though Seth were her son. "Don't you think you're going too fast? You don't want him to faint again! Don't let his head jostle like that!"

"Faint! Boys don't faint, mother, they pass out!" Tyler turned and looked behind them. Sure enough, the daughter was following them too!

"Boy, Seth, you've got the attention of high up people!" Tyler teased quietly. "Even the son-in-law is trailing us!"

"Cut it out, Tyler! Oh, have I got a headache! I've never passed out in my life 'til today, and it just had to happen in front of a hundred people! This is so embarrassing!"

Seth was glad to lie down on his pallet and appreciated the cold rag that was laid on his forehead. He lay there for several minutes ignoring the constant chatter of the Colonel's wife...and his thirty year old daughter...and the mumblings of the son-in-law. He wished they would all just leave.

After about fifteen minutes, Seth sat up, much to the "Mrs. Colonel's" disapproval. "You need to save your strength!"

"I actually need to be helping Dr. Jennings. Thank you for your concern and your help, but I really need to get back to my job. Thanks again!" Without giving her a chance to object, he left the tent.

He hurried over to Dr. Jennings's tent, where the doctor was setting a soldier's arm. Dr. Jennings looked up and smiled. Seth grinned. "Private Seth Mason, reporting for duty, sir!" He decided not to mention his passing out to the doctor or he would get more "treatment."

"Good! Add another piece of wood to the fire. The water ain't boiling yet. I like to keep my things as sterilized as possible, you know." Seth nodded and added the wood. Seth had never heard of boiling water to keep things clean, except when babies were being born.

Well, Dr. Jennings did learn his doctoring from British doctors. Maybe it's a British thing, Seth thought.

"Oh, Dr. Jennings, my Mama, my sister, and her friend arrived last night!"

"That's great! Are they here to help?"

"Yep, they should be here soon." Seth then noticed the soldier's arm. "What happened to you?"

The soldier looked a little embarrassed. "I was kidding around with some of the drummer boys. We were climbing a tree, and I slipped. I broke my arm when I fell."

Dr. Jennings added, "And if you had come straight to me to have it set, I wouldn't have to reset it now." He turned to Seth.

"This happened a few days ago, and it's already started healing crooked."

"I'm sure that hurts," Seth sympathized.

"Uh huh, OUUUCH!" he hollered as the doctor reset his arm. The young man drew in his breath sharply. Dr. Jennings wrapped it securely and then fitted the young man with an arm sling. The soldier soon left.

Before Dr. Jennings could say anything, a messenger came for Seth, saying there were three ladies waiting for him outside the camp.

"That would be the 'volunteers.' Thanks, I'll go see what they need."

Dr. Jennings nodded and started preparing for the next patient. Seth hurried to the outskirts of the camp. Mama, Dixie and Lana were waiting with the wagon of supplies. "Come on, I'll take you to Dr. Hardy, the camp physician. You probably don't want to help Dr. Jennings. He's the surgeon."

"I think you're right," Dixie affirmed. "I don't think my stomach could take that."

"It does get bad sometimes, so we'll leave those jobs to the guys for now." He took over driving the wagon. Mama sat next to him, and the girls sat in the back.

"Seth? What are you doing up?" asked Tyler as he walked alongside the wagon.

"I'm feeling fine now. It ain't like I was dying or anything. Blacking out only takes a little rest." Mama looked at Seth, who quickly explained what had happened. The girls laughed, and Mama just shook her head.

Dr. Hardy was thrilled to have three more helpers and put them to work right away. Mama was to work with David in the sick bay. Lana was going to help Dr. Hardy on his rounds and Dixie was to go from tent to tent, writing letters for the soldiers. Some were too weak or too injured to write their own.

Seth pointed to one of the tents. "This is where you start, so have fun." Dixie looked at her older brother.

"So what do I do? Just walk in and say, 'Hey, what do you want me to write for you?'"

"Not exactly. Umm…introduce yourself, and lead up to your purpose, I guess."

"Thank you *so* much for the advice!" she teased. Seth laughed then headed back to Dr. Jennings' tent.

Dixie looked hesitantly at the tent, and then stepped up to the 'door.' "Um, knock-knock?"

"Come in," came a weak reply. Dixie paused. Then she finally walked in. She glanced around the tent, which contained four wounded soldiers. The one who had called out to her smiled and said, "Hey, who are you?" The man looked about twenty–five years old. He was lying on his pallet, and Dixie couldn't help but notice that he was missing a leg, and his right arm was in a sling.

"I'm Dixianna Mason. Dr. Hardy asked me to see who all needed letters written. Any letters you need written?"

"Yes! Thank you! I need a letter written to my wife. Do you think you could handle that?"

"Yes, of course. Just tell me what you want, and I'll write it."

As Dixie wrote, she couldn't help but get tickled. *This is so mushy! They must really love each other. This reminds me of Mama and Papa!*

The more letters she wrote, the easier it became, although more times than not, she would leave the tents teary eyed. She had never seen that much suffering in her life. At some moments she just wanted to run away from it all, but she also wanted to learn from this.

Walking quickly to the next tent, she checked her paper supply and also consulted the pocket watch Seth was lending her: 11:15. Had she really written ten letters already? She couldn't believe it!

"Knock-knock!"

"Come in," a strong, cheerful voice called.

She pushed open the tent flap and saw the Bowers brothers inside. Nate was lying on his cot, his face flushed with fever. He looked up at Dixie and forced a smile. She could see pain in his eyes and even though he tried, he couldn't hold back a moan.

David finished folding up a blanket and turned toward Dixie. "Hello there! Tie that tent flap back, if you don't mind, Miss," David requested.

After completing the task, David motioned for her to sit down on a wooden crate. "Can we help you with anything, Miss?"

"No, I'm here to help you if you need it. I'm writing letters for anyone who needs me to. I'm Dixianna Mason. My brothers, Richard and Seth, are soldiers here."

Nate nodded and David said, "Oh, yes ma'am, we know Seth. He's been real good to my brother Nate here. I'm David Bowers."

"Seth's told me about y'all. It's good to meet you."

Nate tried to say something, but was stopped by a coughing fit. David quickly grabbed a canteen of water and helped Nate get his cough under control.

He helped Nate into a sitting position. "Nate does need help with a letter. If you'll excuse me, Miss Mason, I need to get back to my rounds." David turned to Nate. "Take it easy, alright?"

Nate nodded and smiled slightly at his brother. David walked out.

"So, you're Nate," Dixie said. "Seth told us about you last night."

"Yep, and I can tell you're Seth's sister," Nate responded, though with much difficulty. "You look just like him."

"Yes, we hear that a lot. You know, you look about the age of my younger brother, Michael. How old are you?"

"Thirteen," he replied, shifting his maimed leg to a more comfortable position."

Dixie smiled at the younger boy. "Michael will be thirteen in November." She glanced around the strangely vacant tent. All the others she had visited had at least four occupants, but Nate was by himself. "Does anyone else tent with you?"

Nate shook his head. "This is Dr. Jennings' tent, and me and my brother share it with him. I can actually rest better away from other people."

"I see. Let's see now, your brother said you needed a letter written. "

"Yes, I do," Nate said. "I need one sent quickly to my Mama." That wasn't unusual; many soldiers were having letters written to their mothers, but the urgency in the younger boy's voice touched Dixie's tender heart.

She forced a smile and said, "Alright, then let's get started. How do you want to open the letter? To your Mother and Father or just your Mother?"

Soon the following letter was placed in Dixie's bag:

Dear Mama,

This is from Nate. I wanted to tell you not to worry about me. I got shot in the leg the day of the battle, and the doctor had to take it. Shortly after that, I was told I had pneumonia and that I probably wouldn't live much longer. I'm not afraid to die. I know where I'm going.

I miss you and Papa Joe terribly bad. Mama, please don't mourn too much when I die. I want you to be glad that I am in heaven with Papa.

Seth Mason is one of my friends here at camp. He's from North Carolina. I met him the day of the amputation. He's a good Christian and is a big encouragement to me. He's been very kind to me. His sister, Dixianna, is helping out with the wounded and is writing this letter for me.

Mama, I love you and Papa Joe. Please remember that verse you always quote, "... Blessed be the name of the Lord," and also "All things work together for good…" I love you.

My Love and Prayers,
Nathan Joseph Bowers

Blinking back tears, Dixie left the tent. *He's comforting his Mother even though he knows he may die soon! No thoughts of bitterness and anger, just love and joy. He's so young!* she thought.

Lord, she prayed silently, *if it be Thy will, spare Nate's life. For his mother's sake, but only if it please Thee to do so. In Jesus' name I pray, Amen.*

★ 1861 ★

"Look at the size of 'em!"

Michael had just landed a huge catfish. Carter congratulated him as he strung it with the other fish. They'd been fishing for most of the afternoon and were ready to head home.

On the way back to the Naces', Carter said, "This has been a lot of fun. It's usually me and Tyler…" Carter stopped suddenly.

Michael knew what he was trying to say. He missed Richard and Seth too. "Thanks for coming with me. I had a great time too. We need to do this again soon."

Carter waded along the pond's edge to the end closest to home. The water felt so good, it was very hot today. Michael splashed along next to him. He looked at his friend. "I guess we'll have to be stand in brothers for each other. Least ways 'til the boys get back."

"Deal!" Carter said with a grin. "Hey, if it's okay with your papa and mine, why don't we pool our fish and you two come over for dinner?"

"If it's alright with your parents, I'm sure Mrs. Bradley would enjoy a night out of the kitchen."

They hurried up to the Naces' place, and Carter showed his parents their catch. He didn't even have to ask his father if they could have the Mason's over; he suggested it before Carter got a chance.

Michael hurried over to ask his father if they could, and before very long, the two families were enjoying the delicious taste of catfish and trout.

★ 1861 ★

Lana ducked into one of the tents with Dr. Hardy. The light coming through the tent flap revealed a man in his mid-thirties. His left leg was in a splint and his right eye was bandaged.

The man smiled. "Hey, Dr. Hardy. Checking on my eye again?"

"Yes, I need to change the bandage." The soldier nodded and the doctor undid the bandage. Lana gasped involuntarily when she saw the eye. It was bloody and infected.

He'll never see out of that eye again! she thought. She shook her head in sympathy, as she handed the doctor a clean, wet rag to clean the wound.

Seeing this, the soldier said, "No worries, Miss. It's all for our country's freedom. God spared the other eye, and I have nothing but thanks to give Him. I can still fight with one eye." Lana smiled and nodded.

She handed Dr. Hardy a jar of what looked like some sort of salve. The soldier flinched as the doctor applied it, but he said nothing.

As they left the tent, Lana was deep in thought. *He's lost an eye but he wants to keep on fighting! He's done his part, but he wants to press on. What an inspiration! What a true Patriot!*

★ 1861 ★

Saturday night, Mama, Lana and Dixie sat around the campfire with Isaac, Richard, Jordan, Seth and Tyler. The boys each held a tin cup of coffee in their hands. The camp was still awake and most sat by their campfires talking and singing.

Dixie glanced at her mother, who nodded. Dixie then said, "We have something in the wagon that I think all of us will enjoy." The boys watched as the girls withdrew three cases. Richard and Seth grinned. It was their guitar, mandolin and fiddle cases. Dixie handed the guitar to Richard and Lana handed Seth his mandolin.

Dixie tuned her fiddle and Lana pulled Tyler's harmonica out of her pocket and passed it to him. Before long, they were enjoying their favorite hymns and folk songs.

The ladies left an hour later, agreeing that the music had been the perfect ending to the day.

 ★1861★

Chapter 16

★

Wrapping Up

My flesh and my heart faileth: but God is the strength of my heart,
and my portion for ever.
Psalm 73:26

Dixie carefully dipped out the soup a local housewife had made. The ladies had attended a camp church service that morning and then had gotten to work.

Dixie carried the soup toward Nate's tent. She knew all the ins and outs of the camp now. Nate was doing worse, and his parents had been sent for. David had been dismissed from his other duties so he could stay with Nate. And since several of the wounded had been evacuated to real hospitals, Seth was able to pop in more frequently.

Seth held the tent flap open for his sister. Dixie set the soup on the crate next to Nate's cot. Mama entered with soup for David and Seth. Mama took Nate's pulse. She frowned, deep in thought, counting. Nate had a fever, and it was starting to climb though he hadn't reached delirium...yet.

David looked at her, wondering what she had found out. Mama motioned for him to step outside with her. "You know more about this than me, Mr. Bowers. What do you think?"

David bit his lip. "I don't think he has much time," he whispered. "I think it will be over today."

Mama nodded, then said, "That's what I'm thinking. If he gets delirious or goes unconscious, will he recover?"

"I doubt it." He looked away.

"I was afraid of that," Mama said, and they stepped back inside. In a low tone, she said to Seth, "See if you can get David to eat some soup. He's set up with him all night and hasn't eaten much."

Seth nodded, unable to speak. Mama and Dixie stepped out of the tent. "I hope his parents get here before…" Mama couldn't finish. Dixie sighed. There was little chance of that. Trains didn't run on Sundays, and unless they had gotten in late last night, they wouldn't be there in time.

Mama hurried away to some other task. Dixie headed off to help Dr. Hardy and was joined by Lana, who made an inquiry on Nate's condition. Dixie relayed the bitter news.

Later on Dixie went back to Nate's tent. Seth was standing next to David, trying to comfort him. At first Dixie thought Nate had passed on, but she soon realized that Nate had slipped into delirium. His eyes were wild with fever. His forehead was very hot.

Dr. Hardy entered the tent with his medical bag. Dixie stepped out with Seth. "He's gonna die, isn't he, Seth?"

"I…I guess so, unless God intervenes. Just keep praying. That's what Nate needs the most right now. God can still heal him if He wants to." He turned his head away.

Dixie looked down. "I'm gonna see if his parents have shown up yet. Jordan's watching the road, so I'm gonna ask him."

"Okay, Dixie."

Before long Dixie had reached the spot where her cousin was working. She was discouraged when she saw he was alone. Jordan turned and saw her. He playfully stood at attention.

"Who goes there? Friend or foe?"

"Friend, you nut. Any sign of Nate's parents?" Jordan shook his head.

140

"How's Nate doing?"

"Not too good. They think it will be over today. He's delirious now. I'm praying hard that Nate's parents will get here in time."

Dixie was about to leave when she heard a horse and buggy coming toward them. The driver was going pretty fast. "Halt!" Jordan ordered. The driver came to a quick stop.

Before Jordan could say anything, the man said, "Please, sir, we're looking for a drummer boy named Nate Bowers. He's our son. We have a telegram telling us to get to camp as soon as possible."

"Go on through. This young lady will show you the way."

"Thank you! Hop on up, Miss." Dixie scrambled up and told him where to go. The man introduced himself as Joe Fane. The lady in the buggy was named Nora; Nate's mother and stepfather. Within minutes Nate's parents were entering his tent.

Nate was unconscious, and his mother knelt next to his cot. Joe put his hand on David's shoulder. David turned and the two were soon embracing. David broke down as Joe started praying in a whisper. Dixie had already left, and Seth started to back out of the tent, but Nate's mother motioned for him to stay.

Seth listened to Nate's breathing pattern and noticed that it wasn't as strained as before. He was breathing easier. Seth hesitantly placed his hand on his forehead. It was cooler! He counted Nate's pulse rate. It was starting to level out to its normal rate.

Seth quickly left in search of Dr. Hardy. He soon found him. "Dr. Hardy, come quick! Nate's fever's cooling down!" He left the doctor's tent and went in search of Chaplain Davis. Dr. Hardy hurried to Nate's tent, and the chaplain and Seth were close behind.

Mama hurried to the edge of the tent with Dixie at her heels. Seth hurried over to them and explained what was going on.

As Dr. Hardy began his examination, Nate's eyes fluttered opened. David looked surprised. Seth stepped closer to see if he really was awake. His mother gently touched her youngest son's forehead. "Mama? Papa Joe? What are y'all doing here? What's going on?"

While his mother explained, the doctor listened to his breathing and heartbeat. Chaplain Davis prayed as the doctor examined and re-examined Nate.

When the chaplain said amen, Dr. Hardy said, "I don't understand this. Less than fifteen minutes ago, I checked on this boy, and he was nearing the pearly gates. But now? I think he's gonna make it!"

"Praise the Lord!" exclaimed Joe. Nora, crying tears of joy could only nod her thanks as she hugged her son. Dr. Hardy helped Nate sit up. David was overwhelmed with gratitude to God for sparing his brother's life.

Seth grabbed Dixie and hugged her in his excitement. Mama's eyes were brimming with tears of gratitude for sparing Nate's family the loss of a son.

Nora was helping Nate sip some of the soup that had been brought to him earlier. Dixie left to tell Lana and Jordan what had happened. She was in awe of the miracle God had performed right before her eyes. God had answered "Yes" to their prayers.

★ 1861 ★

Michael was lying across his bed, rereading Seth's letter for the third time that day. He was just finishing when Papa walked into his room. Michael looked up. "Hey, Papa. Need something?"

"Yep, sure do. Think me and you could talk for a few minutes?"

"Sure." Michael tried to think of something his father would need to talk to him about. Not that Papa never talked with him privately, but there was something in his voice that made Michael wonder if something was wrong.

"Michael, you're my son. I promised God when you were born that I would raise you to be a good Christian boy.

You've known the Lord as your Savior for about six years now, right?"

"Right."

"Well, in order for me to keep my promise, I need to bring something to your attention. I've noticed that you've developed an attitude toward the Union soldiers. There's nothing wrong with supporting the Confederates, cheering a Southern victory or even saying the South is right and the North is wrong. But it is wrong to get excited over Union casualties. I know that casualties include wounded and missing in action, but many casualties are deaths.

"Think of them as souls, Michael. You shouldn't *want* the Yankees to get hurt. Yes, I know that's hard because we're fighting them, but remember, the South tried to keep war from happening. So what if the Yankees are wrong? They still need Jesus, just like everyone else. We *do* know that some are Christians. There are good and bad Yankees, Michael. Some honestly think they're doing what's right, but many of them have no idea why they're fighting.

"I don't want to see the seed of hatred take root in your heart, Michael. When we hate something or someone, we can't grow spiritually. Why don't you try praying for the Yankees? Pray that they come to their senses before more lives are lost."

Michael hung his head. "I'm sorry, Papa. You're right, my attitude was wrong. I'll pray for God to forgive me, and then pray for the Yanks to figure out that they need to let things go. I need to be careful, even when I pray for them though. I might get in the wrong spirit about it. Thanks for talking with me."

"You're welcome, son. Why don't we pray together right now for God to help us?"

"Sure."

★ 1861 ★

It was decided that Nate would return home with his parents on Monday, since Joe was a doctor and could care for him at home. Nate seemed happy, but David and Seth knew

143

something was wrong. They soon found out what was wrong the next time they were alone with him.

No sooner had they entered the tent, than he said, "Why? Why did God let me live? I was so close! I wanted to go home so bad, but God let me live. Why?" David looked at Seth for an answer. Seth prayed for wisdom.

"Well...I really can't answer that, Nate, because I don't know. Maybe God has some special task He wants you to do for Him. But one thing I do know is that God saved your brother through all this. And God helped David accept your father's death. God has a reason for everything He does, Nate."

David spoke up. "Me and Papa Joe have talked, Nate, and now, I think we can have a proper relationship. God works in very mysterious ways."

The boys talked for a while. After a bit, Nate fell silent, and then said, "Can I ask a favor? I've been in here ever since the amputation. Could y'all help me outside just for a little while?"

"Sure," they said together. They helped the weak boy out of bed. Color was coming back to Nate's face. Seth held him up while David got Nate's crutches. Seth hadn't realized how tall Nate was. He was nearly as tall as Seth!

After teaching Nate how to use the crutches the three emerged from the tent. Nate drank in the sights that had been hidden from him for so long. Joe and Nora watched as the boys helped Nate take halting steps around the tent. Tears flowed freely down Nora's cheeks. "Thank you, Lord," she whispered.

Joe hugged her tightly. "He's moving forward, Nora. His leg won't stop him, he's moving on."

★ 1861 ★

Monday came, and Nate and his parents left. Seth had only known him for a short while, yet it was hard to see his friend leave. Knowing he wasn't leaving in death helped though. Nate waved as the carriage left the camp.

Shortly thereafter, the boys from Jackson's brigade were informed that they were to leave the next morning to escort the wounded to Richmond, then return to their home brigade. The boys were excited. In a few days they'd be heading back to their brigade, the "Stonewall Brigade," as a few had nicknamed it.

David was going with them as well. He'd been given an assignment to work in a military hospital in Richmond. He was glad for this, for he'd be near his family and he'd be able to work with professional doctors every day to enhance his training.

The girls meantime had started packing up empty crates and things they had brought. They were leaving in the morning to return home after two weeks of helping in the camps. They would miss both family and friends, but they couldn't deny the fact that they were ready to head home.

★ 1861 ★

That evening, before lights out, Richard picked a nameless, very mournful sounding tune on his guitar. Dixie noticed that he was repeating a series of chords over and over. She picked up the tune on her fiddle, adding a little bit here and there. Tyler played a few notes on the harmonica. Seth was showing Jordan some chords on the mandolin. Mama and Lana listened to the interesting array of sounds. The "music" stopped momentarily.

Dixie realigned her fiddle, and began playing a familiar song. The boys joined her as she played, "*What Wondrous Love is this?*" Lana's lone voice began to sing.

> "*What wondrous love is this, oh my soul, oh my soul?*
> *What wondrous love is this oh my soul?*
> *What wondrous love is this that caused the Lord of bliss,*
> *To bare the dreadful curse for my soul, for my soul?*
> *To bare the dreadful curse for my soul?*"

They skipped the middle two verses and played the final verse, raising it one octave, and other voices joined in.

"And when from death I'm free, I'll sing on, I'll sing on.
And when from death I'm free, I'll sing on.
And when from death I'm free, I'll sing and joyful be!
And through eternity, I'll sing on, I'll sing on.
And through eternity, I'll sing on."

 ★1861★

Chapter 17

★

Home At Last

...He blesseth the habitation of the just.
Proverbs 3:33

"I miss them already."

Mama turned and smiled sympathetically at her daughter. Dixie was referring to her brothers. That morning the ladies had left for North Carolina.

The train chugged along the tracks with their rhythmic click clacks. Dixie was skimming a newspaper. "Here we go; this is what I've been looking for." Dixie carefully tore the article out of the newspaper. Then she removed two books from her homemade bag. One was the journal her parents had given her for her birthday; the other was a blank book she had bought.

She reached into her bag and withdrew a small jar of paste. She opened the second book, flipped past other article filled pages until she came to a blank page and carefully pasted the new article in.

Lana looked over at her strangely. Dixie explained, "I'm pasting articles about the war in this book. I have one about Fort Sumter, some about secession, the war breaking out, and now about Manassas Junction. I want to make a keepsake for future generations so they won't forget what happened to their ancestors.

"In my journal I'm writing about my family's personal experiences during the war. I wrote down stories Richard and Seth told me, plus some of my own about volunteering. I'm writing exactly how I feel about everything that's happening. Michael is doing the same. I think it is so important for future generations to understand what really happened years before. I wonder if my ancestors did anything like that…"

Lana looked excited. "That's a good idea, Dixie. I want to do that too! I have a journal at home, but I haven't written in it yet. You always have such good ideas."

"Thank you. It was your idea to bring the instruments with us on this trip. I'm glad we did. That was one of my favorite parts of this trip, sitting around the camp fire, singing and playing songs…I won't forget it."

Dixie looked out the window, thinking of her older brothers. Mama also thought of her sons and their friends. She smiled at the memories of the past few weeks.

The trip was a pleasant one. Dixie could barely believe that in a short time, she would be home!

★ 1861 ★

"Hey, Papa! Mama and Dixie's home!" Michael yelled from his favorite tree. He jumped down and raced toward the wagons. He reached Mama first, hugging her so tightly you'd have thought he hadn't seen her in years. She returned his hug as Papa and the Bradleys joined the group.

After the general excitement had died down, Michael tapped Dixie's shoulder to get her attention. "Peek-a-boo had seven kittens in the barn loft! Come and see them!" Dixie and Michael headed for the loft.

The kittens were adorable! The mama, a tortoise shell, seemed proud to show off her babies to her guests.

After playing with the kittens, they all headed in for some fresh apple pie that Mrs. Bradley had made. The guys wanted to hear about the trip, so Mama and Dixie told them in between bites. Dixie didn't leave out any details.

She told them about the suffering but also how everyone seemed to have such a strong sense of patriotism. She told them about their times around the campfire. Mama's green eyes were moist as they rehashed the miraculous story of Nate's recovery.

"But this war isn't over yet. We still have to convince the Yankees that they are beaten," Dixie sighed in conclusion.

"Dixie," Papa said, "I'm so proud of you for sacrificing your time and energy to do what God wanted you to do. I think you've learned a lot in the past two weeks. You and Lana did a woman's job. I'm proud of you." He winked at his wife. "The same goes for you." Mama just laughed.

Papa hugged his daughter. Her father's words meant more to her than all the money in the world. She didn't feel that she had made a great sacrifice, but it was good to be home.

As Dixie drifted off to sleep, she wondered what her Northern family was up to. A few tears slid down her cheeks as she thought of her cousins who were unsaved. She also cried over the knowledge that Philip, Charles, Drew and Allen had all joined the Union forces. She'd known for a while, but it still pained her to know that eventually Richard and Seth would more than likely be fighting against them.

Allen Cameron had joined in Gettysburg, Pennsylvania, but Drew Cameron had joined in Philadelphia with Philip Rains and Charles Tinderman, so the three were together. Dixie wondered if they had been at Manassas Junction. She hoped not.

Dear Lord, She prayed silently, *Please save Charles, Christopher and Constance Angelica. And please keep the others safe. Protect them, Lord. Please…*

★ 1861 ★

Philip Rains wearily laid down his rifle. He had been on patrol all night. He dropped down on a log near the camp fire. Drew Cameron walked up to him and handed him a cup of

149

coffee. Philip smiled as he drank the warm drink. "Thank you, Drew."

"You're welcome." Drew sat down next to his cousin. "Did you see any Rebels?"

"Two. I think they were scouts. Charles and some others went after them. That was about 7:30 yesterday evening. My relief man went with them, so I had patrol all night." His voice dropped to a whisper. "They took two dogs with them."

Drew shuddered. "I can't stand those blood hounds." Before Philip could reply, there was a shout at the camp's entrance, followed by a great commotion. The cousins stood and walked toward the mass of soldiers, to see what was going on.

They saw Charles Tinderman in the group and waved him over to them. Charles removed his dark blue kepi and wiped sweat off his forehead. He smiled brightly at his cousins. His whole body seemed to tremble with excitement. "We caught one! The other one got away, but we caught one!"

Philip grinned, but Drew had a question. "Did you let the dogs loose?"

Charles laughed at his cousin's concern. "We let them loose, but they didn't hurt the Rebs too badly. The Rebel we caught has a lot of bites and cuts on his arm, but not bad enough to make it useless. That's it, no more, no less."

Drew breathed a sigh of relief. "Good. I cannot stand the thought of someone getting mauled by a blood hound." Charles rolled his eyes, and Philip shrugged.

"The best part is that we have good reason to believe that he is with a group rejoining General Jackson's brigade. He might have some important information we could use!"

Since it was about 6:00 in the morning, Capt. Horner told Philip and the others that had been up all night to go to bed while others were sent to search for the other Confederates that surely were in the area.

Philip stumbled into bed, but Charles had a little trouble going to sleep. His adrenalin was up and it was going to take him awhile.

Chapter 18

★

Prayer Works

*Send thine hand from above; rid me and deliver me out of great
waters, from the hand of strange children;*
Psalm 144:7

D rew was told to guard the prisoner and see if he could get
him to talk. The young man's arm was still bleeding
profusely, and it was obvious that no one was going to do
anything about it. The young Rebel was trembling, partly from
pain, partly from fear. Drew couldn't stand to see anyone suffer,
not even an enemy. He asked the doctor to see to the Reb's arm,
but was refused.

After several minutes of bantering, the doctor finally
gave Drew some bandages for the boy's wounds. Drew then
proceeded to untie the boy's hands from behind his back and
carefully clean and bandage the wounds. The Confederate
looked at him with a confused look on his face, as though he
didn't understand why Drew was helping him.

Drew's face showed his concern. "Does it hurt bad?"

The southerner was reluctant to talk to a blue coat. He
just shook his head. Drew finished tying off the bandage and
retied the boy's hands in front. He tried to think of some way to

get the prisoner into a conversation. "Um...do you think the battle over at Bull Run will be the end of the fighting?"

The young man just stared hard at Drew, studying his face. Drew raised his eyebrows. "What?" The boy looked down at his shoes.

Drew sighed. "You're not much for talking are you?"

"Not to Yankees," the boy mumbled.

"Can't we lay our politics aside and just have a conversation with each other?"

The prisoner's eyes flashed. "It ain't politics, it's morals; and no, it can't be laid aside! You're a Yankee invader, and I'm a southern defender. No, we can't have a conversation!" With that he fell silent and refused to speak no matter how much Drew coaxed him.

"Look, I have family that supports the Confederacy. They're fine people. But just because we disagree doesn't mean we'd never speak civilly to each other again. Why can't you and I?"

Another Yankee soldier walked up. "Pvt. Cameron, if you're going to get anywhere with him, you have to be more aggressive. Don't coddle him."

Drew looked up. "And you could do a better job?"

The soldier smirked. "I can get him to talk. I might have to rough him up some, but he'd sure talk when I got done." The prisoner looked up at the new comer with wide eyes.

Drew glared at the soldier. "He's in *my* charge," he said, standing and handling his gun in a threating way. "Get out of here."

The prisoner looked up at Drew in surprise. The other Yank scowled and backed away. Drew sat back down across from his charge. The boy looked him square in the eye, once again studying him. This time Drew said nothing but let the young man look.

At last he looked away, but he didn't seem quite so nervous now. Drew debated on whether to try and strike up a conversation once more. "So why are you fighting? What's your reason for joining the Confederate army?"

The young man looked up. A hint of a smile played at his lips. "Do you have time for me to explain all that?"

Drew nodded. "I have plenty of time."

"Alright. Here's how it is…"

★ 1861 ★

Levi Andrews ran as fast as he could toward the makeshift Confederate camp. He was gasping for breath. Seth took one look at him and knew he'd been attacked by some sort of animal. His face was gashed and bleeding. Seth acted as a doctor and applied pressure to the young Jewish man's wounds in attempt to stop the bleeding.

The small group of soldiers gathered around for an explanation. They had left Richmond two days before and were returning to their home base. They hadn't broken camp for the day yet, but now something was wrong. After catching his breath, Levi related what happened.

"Me and Jeremy were looking for something to shoot for supper like y'all asked us to. We were a good ways away from here when we were spotted by some Union sentries. We ran, and they followed us with a couple blood hounds. The hounds caught up with us and tripped us up. That's where these scratches came from.

"I finally got the one off of me, and I shot at the one on Jeremy. I didn't kill it, but it bought us some time. But they were still gaining on us. Jeremy and I knew we'd have to split up if either of us were going to get back to camp in one piece. He chose to be the one to distract the Yanks so I could get back here.

"The Yanks followed him, and I headed for here as quick as I could. A few of them followed me, but they lost me at the creek. I hid and decided to follow them. I found their camp by doing so." He paused. "They caught Jeremy. Don't know how. There are quite a few Yankees there. It would be a near impossibility to get Jeremy out of there."

Alvin sat down on a stump, his brow knit as he thought over what he had just heard. Richard spoke first. "How many Yankees do you think are there?"

Levi thought a moment. "Not even a full company. Maybe thirty or thirty five soldiers."

Richard nodded. "Eight to thirty-five ain't a fair fight. I think we should keep an eye on the camp and see what happens," suggested Isaac. "Prayer will help the situation."

The others agreed except for Titus Mallory.

"Why waste our time? It won't do any good. Never has, never will. Why bother?"

Seth looked at Titus in surprise. How could he say such a thing? He knew Titus didn't profess to be a follower of Jesus, but Seth hadn't detected his bitterness until now.

Jordan quietly said, "Prayer worked for Nate Bowers when he was sick. It helped us win Manassas. It-"

"STOP! I don't want to hear it! It didn't help my brother any! It didn't! Don't you dare tell me prayer works!" Titus shouted. Jordan stepped back, for Titus looked like he was going to punch him.

The others looked at each other in shock as Titus wheeled around and stormed away. Richard rubbed the back of his neck. "Okay, what just happened here? All we were going to do was stop and pray, and he goes crazy!"

Levi bit his lip. "He's real upset about a letter he just got. His older brother was arrested a few months back because he printed the truth in his newspaper. He lived up north and he was a preacher.

"When the conflict started, he printed exactly what happened, not what the Yankees tried to bribe him to print. When he wouldn't back down to their threats, they told the police that he was trying to start an uprising. They paid people to 'back up' the story."

Levi shook his head. "This last letter from his sister said that he's still in prison. He says prayer hasn't helped his brother at all. And he has a wife and three young children."

Richard and Seth exchanged concerned glances. "How do you know all this?" Richard asked.

Levi laughed a little. "I tent with him, and I made the mistake of asking how his family was doing. At first he only told me his brother was in jail on false charges. Then I said I'd be praying for him, and Titus blew up at me and told me everything."

Isaac considered what they had just been told. "Why don't we stop and pray for the Mallory family right now. Sounds like they could sure use it.

The boys knelt in a circle to pray. They prayed for Titus's salvation and that somehow God would use his brother's situation to bring him to Christ. They also prayed for wisdom as to what to do about Jeremy. They prayed for his protection and for him to have God's strength during this time.

Isaac spoke first. "I think we should just wait here for a couple days watching the camp. Maybe we can find a way to sneak Jeremy out of the camp."

★ 1861 ★

"...So if you were in our situation, what would you have done? Just stood by and let soldiers from another country come in and take you captive? Y'all invaded us. We have the right to defend ourselves."

Drew sat for a moment in silence, thinking over what Jeremy had just said. "You sure do paint an ugly picture of us. I guess I sort of understand how you would think of us like that...but it isn't like that at all. We just want to remain a united country. We fought the British twice to establish this country, and you guys are tearing apart all that hard work. Can't you understand how we feel?"

Jeremy shook his head. "We're just doing what the Patriots did in the face of tyranny."

Drew sighed and looked away. He wasn't getting anywhere with his prisoner. It was afternoon. Jeremy wondered what his fellow soldiers were doing now. He hoped the Yanks wouldn't discover their camp! He wondered if Levi was alright.

The afternoon slowly turned into evening. Drew had tried to keep small talk going, but no heated, or important, discussions were taken up. Time seemed to drag.

Jeremy glanced around the camp. At last it was starting to get dark and soldiers were already retiring to their tents. Even the soldiers who'd been sent to search for other Confederate troops had returned…empty handed.

All during their conversation, Jeremy had kept his eyes open for a chance to escape. He cringed inwardly at the thought of having to hurt Drew since he'd been so kind. But Drew was still the enemy, and Jeremy had to take the opportunity to run if it presented itself.

Lord, help me overpower this guy and get out of here. I need Your help right now, Lord, Jeremy prayed silently. *He's been so nice. I really don't want to hurt him. Oh, Lord, help me make the right decision!* Jeremy had never struggled like this before.

Drew reached up to scratch his head and knocked his hat off in the process. Sighing, he reached down to retrieve it. He relaxed his grip on his gun for a split second; that was all Jeremy needed.

He kicked the stool Drew was sitting on, knocking him to the ground and sending the gun flying out of his hands. Jeremy took off for the woods. He'd just entered the shelter of the trees when Drew had recovered from his shock and shouted, "Call out the guards! The prisoner's loose!"

Jeremy ran for all he was worth. With his hands bound, escaping would be that much harder. He could hear the dogs baying and a couple shots were fired. His heart was pounding like a drum.

He tripped over a rock and went sprawling to the ground. Jeremy struggled to regain his footing and took off again.

Bang!

A bullet suddenly bit into his already injured arm. Jeremy bit his lip to keep from hollering and giving away his position.

Just when it seemed the Yanks were going to catch up with him, he spotted a river flowing gently along a tree line. Taking a deep breath, Jeremy slipped into the water and hid himself under a bush leaning over the bank on the other side of the river, concealing him from view.

Gasping for air, Jeremy rested under his foliage haven. He heard the Yanks approaching the opposite bank with the dogs. "He came this way for sure. There's blood on the bank here. And there are ripples in the water."

Jeremy once again held his breath.

The soldiers were beating the bushes on their side of the bank, jabbing them with their bayonets. He could hear them wading across the river to his side. *Lord, help me!* he cried out silently.

"Cameron, you're going to be in big trouble, letting the prisoner outsmart you like that! The captain's not going to be happy at all."

Jeremy could barely see Drew in the dim light. Drew looked worried. "I didn't try to lose him. He caught me off guard."

The first soldier sneered. "That's what you get for being nice to Rebels. They play it nice and hit you when you least expect it. He had you right where he wanted you."

"Enough talk. Keep looking for the Reb," a sergeant barked.

They began beating the bushes around Jeremy and jabbing them in like manner. Jeremy gasped as a blade barely missed his face, but the soldiers were making too much noise to hear him.

At last, the soldiers moved on. Jeremy let out his breath slowly. He moved cautiously out from under his hiding place. It was almost completely dark now and Jeremy had no clue where he was. He didn't want to risk running into the Yanks in the dark, so he pulled himself out of the water and onto the bank, hiding in the full bushes.

It was rough sleeping that night; every noise startled Jeremy awake, and at one point he heard the Yankees doubling back from their fruitless search. They crossed the river without stumbling across Jeremy's hiding spot.

Lord, he prayed silently, *I can't get anywhere in the dark. Please let me get some rest so I can get ahead of the Yanks tomorrow. I've got to get some sleep! Help me to move forward in Your strength.*

God answered his prayer and before long, Jeremy was fast asleep.

Just as the sun was rising the next morning, Jeremy woke up. Knowing the Yanks would be looking for him again today, Jeremy tried to get free from his rope bonds. He twisted his hands, trying to loosen them, but he was only rewarded with raw wrists.

Next he tried undoing the knots with his teeth, but they were too tight; Drew was too good of a knot-tier. Trying to get his bearings, Jeremy glanced at the moss on the trees. By that he could tell where the cardinal directions were. He headed southeast, the direction he and the others had been going before. He hoped to run into them…and away from the enemy camp.

Jeremy prayed silently that the Yanks wouldn't find him or the others for that matter. They'd really be in a fix then! He kept going, hunger gnawing at him. He could get water from the river, but food was another story.

By noon, Jeremy was exhausted and hopelessly lost in the woods. He sank down to the ground to rest against a tree. Lifting his gaze heavenward, he once again prayed for help and strength to go on.

Snap!

Jeremy jumped in surprise. Where had the noise come from? He hurried to conceal himself in some shrubs nearby. He could hear footsteps coming closer and closer. From his prone position, he could now see a mud covered boot…now a white pant leg. Jeremy shifted so he could see the whole intruder. He sighed with relief.

"Cpl. Mallory!"

Titus jerked his head in the direction of the voice and aimed his gun. "Come out!" he ordered.

Jeremy scrambled to his feet and joined his friend in the clearing. Titus looked like he'd seen a ghost. "Jeremy Calling! What are you doing out here? Oh, what happened to your arm?"

"Long story. Is the camp nearby?" Jeremy asked as Titus cut the ropes that bound his wrists.

"Sure is. Come on. The others will be glad to see you. We've been worried sick!"

When they reached the camp, exclamations of delight were made, praising God for delivering their friend. Titus just rolled his eyes at this. Seth quickly set to work doctoring Jeremy's arm.

"Jeremy, how'd you get out of there?" asked Alvin.

Jeremy related the turn of events, ending with, "God said yes to my prayers, and I know y'all were praying for me. At first I was so jumpy, but I remembered that I wasn't alone, and God gave me peace that everything was gonna be fine."

Richard had listened carefully to the account. "I think it's wonderful how God used Mallory to help you back here. That sure was perfect timing."

Jeremy nodded in agreement. "If God hadn't sent him by, I'd still be walking circles out there."

"I guess that makes you the hero, Mallory," one of the fellows said.

"Don't go calling me a hero for just stumbling across a lost soldier," Titus replied as he walked away.

"Well, let's not sit here for the rest of the day!" Isaac said excitedly. "Richard, get Jeremy something to eat. Then, let's break camp and move out."

When they finally hit the trail, Titus mulled over the whole incident from start to finish. *Prayer! Hero! Seems to me Calling was just plain lucky! But I must admit, that part about peace sure has me stumped...*

★1861★

Chapter 19
★
Hide 'n Seek and Nicodemus

And I will cleanse them from all their iniquity, whereby they have sinned against me;
Jeremiah 33:8a

Annie Nace and Dixie looked out the window where they could see their siblings playing. The window seat was their favorite place to read or do needlework. It was Saturday, and Annie and Dixie were enjoying some quiet time while working their needles.

Kathie Nace was mending Carter's overalls on the sofa, and Jonathan was tending some indigo plants. Annie looked down at her sampler. She was stitching a picture of a harvested indigo plant surrounded by green leaves. Then, in a circle around the picture were the words, *"The Nace Family Indigo Packing and Shipping Co."* When finished, the sampler would be hung in her father's study.

Dixie's was a nine square patchwork sampler. One represented her father, and the others represented his siblings, including their full name, birthdate, and something they liked. It was a gift for her grandparents.

Annie looked over at Dixie's needle work. "Dixie, that's so pretty! I think I'll do one like that next time."

Dixie grinned. "I can't take the credit for it. I got the idea from a friend. She calls it a 'hobby quilt'."

"It's so cute! I'd have to do ours a little different...There's not quite enough Naces!"

Kathie laughed at the comment and looked out the window. "Aren't you two getting tired of that needle work? You've been working on it ever since dinner. Maybe you'd rather go outside."

"I don't think I could ever tire of needle work. I could do it all day. I guess I got used to it since we didn't go outside much when we lived in Baltimore."

Kathie smiled at her daughter. Annie had felt more at home in Baltimore than any of the other Naces. Although she loved Four Tree Springs, Kathie knew she missed her old home.

"Why don't we take our work outside? There's a nice breeze blowing," suggested Dixie. The others quickly agreed.

Upon reaching the outdoors, they found the children playing hide and seek. "Annie, Dixie come play!" Alyssa Rose called, and the others soon picked up the plea.

Annie grinned. "Why not?" They quickly joined them as Alyssa Rose was declared "it."

Carter scrambled up into the high branches of a poplar tree. Annie lay down inside an old dry watering trough.

Dixie, adventurous one that she was, hid in the barn rafters, carefully balancing herself so that jumping down would be easy. Michael laughed at his sister and darted toward the feed room.

After counting to fifty, Alyssa Rose headed toward the woods and then dashed over to the barn. Michael was quickly discovered.

Dixie waited until they were out of ear shot, then she jumped down and hid in the feed room, knowing it wouldn't be searched again.

Meanwhile, Alyssa Rose had discovered Carter's hiding spot. "Okay, we just need Annie and Dixie," she declared.

"Have fun finding them," Carter said. "They're the hardest to find."

"We'll find them. I know we will!" Alyssa Rose said determinedly. "I'll search the smoke house. Michael will search the woods again and Carter will search the yard hiding places. Come on! Let's go!"

Michael swept off his hat and bowed. "Our pleasure, m'lady." Laughing the boys headed off.

Annie wouldn't have been found had she not had a sneezing fit just as Carter walked past. Poor Annie's hay fever hadn't gone away yet. Her mother had given her an herbal tea earlier, and though it had helped, it hadn't eliminated the sneezing…yet.

Dixie eventually came out of hiding, after everyone gave up. She was once again the victor!

As Annie recovered from her sneezing fit, she thought of Tyler and where he was at that moment. She missed her older brother terribly. Every time she thought of him, she stopped and prayed for him. She did so now, then went inside with the others for some cold lemonade.

★ 1861 ★

And the Lord knew Tyler needed her prayers, for at that very moment he was being treated for a snake bite. They had just arrived at General Jackson's brigade, though this wasn't the way they had expected to celebrate.

The doctor stood up and said, "Alright, now tell me again what happened, *slowly*."

Tyler took a deep breath and began the explanation. "We had stopped at a creek to water the horses and fill our canteens. I was filling mine, and the next thing I knew, the snake had come and bit me. We got here as fast as possible. We were glad the camp wasn't far away."

The doctor looked troubled. "So, does anyone know what kind of snake it was?"

Alvin Willis nodded. "It was a copperhead." He quickly described the snake to the doctor.

"That does sound like a copperhead," the doctor agreed. "You should be fine now, although any snake bite can make you sick, maybe even sick to your stomach, if you know what I mean." Tyler nodded.

The doctor turned to Levi. Levi and Jeremy still bore signs of the dogs' attack days earlier. "What happened to your face? Let me take a look at it." After Levi's face had been cared for, and Jeremy's arm checked, the boys reported to their superior officer who reassigned them to their different campsites.

Richard greeted his friends as he settled back in and was soon swapping stories about the last couple of weeks.

Seth and Tyler, meanwhile, were getting acquainted with new tent mates, Joshua Kinston and Lewis Nelson. Joshua, who wanted to be a doctor someday, was very interested in Tyler's snake story. Seth and Lewis were discussing the battle at Manassas. "I think fighting would be much easier if our loading process wasn't so tedious!" Lewis commented.

Seth nodded. "It *is* kinda nerve racking. What would be even better is if you could fire more than one shot at a time."

Lewis grinned. "I think that would be great! Who knows maybe they will someday. I know it's been attempted, but I'm not sure if it worked."

"I doubt it," Seth objected, "or the Yanks would be using them."

Lewis agreed with Seth's observation.

"Roll Call!" bellowed an officer. The boys snapped to attention and hurried off for the "head count." Tyler was excused from the count since he was already feeling the effects of the snake bite.

Isaac and Levi stood next to each other in the lineup. A man stepped out of one of the tents. Isaac's eyes widened. It was Stonewall Jackson himself! Although he'd never seen the general before, Richard had described him well, and Isaac knew it was him.

After roll call General Jackson strolled over toward the woods. "Now there's a man who cares about his men," said a sergeant standing nearby.

"Yes," replied another. "Goes out there and prays for the troops at least twice a day, probably more."

Isaac smiled to himself and silently thanked God for giving them such a good general. "We're in good hands."

★ 1861 ★

Sunday services in camp were a bit different than a regular service. Two younger soldiers played the music with a fiddle and harmonica. The group sang along with the familiar tunes.

Richard and Seth were thrilled that Titus had agreed to come to the services. Maybe today Titus would get saved!

The sermon was preached with fervor by a deep voiced chaplain. "Plain and Simple Salvation," was his sermon title.

"Salvation," he began, "is the most important decision you will ever make. Please turn in your Bibles to John 3:1-16." He proceeded to read the passage. "Let us pray."

The congregation bowed their heads and the chaplain prayed. "Our Father in heaven, we pray that You will grant us the knowledge to rightly understand Your word. Please guard my lips so that only what will please You will be spoken. Please stir our hearts. Bless those here today. Please bring this war to a swift end. Protect and guide us in the days to come. We'll thank You and do thank You for it. In Christ's name I pray, Amen."

The preacher began, "As we all know, our country is engaged in a war. Some are calling it a 'Civil War.' The first time I heard that, I thought, 'What's so civil about war?' Well, the phrase, 'Civil War,' means that two forces that are citizens of the same country, are fighting against each other.

"Now this statement isn't exactly true. The North says it is a civil war because the South is in 'rebellion,' but is still part of the Union. The South says that according to the recent secessions, we are a separate country. I don't know who's right on the definition, but I know which cause seems to be the righteous one."

Members of the congregation glanced at each other and nodded in agreement. Tyler suppressed a laugh, and he saw the corners of Seth's mouth twitching into a smile.

"No don't get me wrong," the preacher continued. "I wish we weren't at war, and I wish we were still one nation. But, since the North wouldn't negotiate, I think God's hand is on the Confederacy. But we must remember, that even though the Northern soldiers are our enemy, there are still good Christians among them. The Christians in their ranks are our brothers in Christ. Let's try to keep this in mind during the war. Pray for the Northerners. Pray for God's will to be done."

Richard nodded his agreement. He had his Yankee cousins on his mind. Charles wasn't saved, and Richard prayed every day for his conversion.

"I trust y'all will never forget the battle that took place at Manassas Junction. When I heard about it, the Lord put a burden on my heart...a burden for souls. People go out into eternity at an alarming rate and even more so during a war. God laid this sermon on my heart and I pray it will be a blessing and a help to you."

"In this passage, we read about Nicodemus's conversation with Jesus. I want to show you three things quickly, then I'll be done. First, I want to look at the Sinner's Countenance. In verse one we read, *'There was a man of the Pharisees, named Nicodemus, a ruler of the Jews:'*

"Nicodemus was, as we all are, a sinner. He wanted some answers to his questions. But he begins with a statement. Verse two says, *'The same came to Jesus by night, and said unto him, Rabbi, we know that thou art a teacher come from God: for no man can do these miracles that thou doest, except God be with him.'*

"In this statement we find that he believed that Jesus was sent of God, but he thought Jesus was only a teacher, a good moral man. But Jesus is more than that! He is the Messiah! Jesus is about to answer with a surprising speech.

"Verse three: *'Jesus answered and said unto him, Verily, verily, I say unto thee, Except a man be born again, he cannot see the kingdom of God.'*

"You may think, 'What does that have to do with anything? Nicodemus didn't mention the Kingdom of God.' Allow me to remind you that Jesus was 100% man and 100% God. He knew what was in Nicodemus's heart. He knew Nicodemus wanted to know about this matter.

"This tells us a few things about this sinner. We know he is a Pharisee and a ruler of the Jews. He was a man of authority. Remember, this is the group of people who would later have Jesus put to death. Because of a verse in John 19, I don't think Nicodemus had anything to do with that. John 19:39 says, *'And there came also Nicodemus, which at the first came to Jesus at night, and brought a mixture of myrrh and aloes, about an hundred pound weight.'*"

This surprised Tyler. He didn't know Nicodemus was mentioned again in the Bible. *Jesus must have made quite an impression on Nicodemus for him to bring those spices to His burial,* he thought.

"Next, we find that Nicodemus knew Jesus came from a Higher Authority. Even though he may not have realized Jesus' full capacity, he did realize that Jesus was *'a teacher come from God,'* and that He was to be respected. He wasn't afraid to admit that Jesus was higher than himself. In another passage, some Pharisees said that Jesus preformed miracles in Satan's name. I don't know about you, but I think that falls under the unpardonable sin of blaspheming the Holy Spirit. Jesus was sent by God!"

"Amen!" was heard all over the congregation.

"The second thing I want you to notice is the Savior's Conversation. In verses 3-16, Jesus explains the concept of salvation. His conversation was pure and holy. He wasn't talking about the latest juicy piece of gossip. He was talking about the most important decision anyone would ever make."

The preacher read through verse 15, then paused and flashed a big smile. "This next verse is salvation up one side and down the other. In fact, it ties together point two and point three, which is Salvation's Concept. Listen to this verse very carefully. *'For God so loved the world, that he gave his only begotten Son, that whosoever believeth in him should not perish, but have everlasting life.'*

"Doesn't that thrill you, Christian, to know that God did that for you? And doesn't it thrill you, lost ones, that He loves you and wants to save you? All you have to do is admit you are a sinner, believe that Jesus Christ will save you from an eternity in a burning hell, and that He died for your sins and rose again on the third day. Confess that you are a sinner, ask for forgiveness, and accept Him as your Savior. That's it! That's salvation, plain and simple salvation. Won't you come and accept Him as your Savior today?"

The musicians began playing the invitation and the soldiers sang in low tones, *"Come, Ye Sinners, Poor and Needy."* Titus stood as still as a mountain, unmovable. This sermon wasn't going to affect him, or so he thought. Inside him, a battle was raging fiercer than the Battle of Manassas Junction.

Titus started sweating. Isaac noticed and nudged Richard, who was standing next to Titus. Conviction revealed itself in Titus' countenance. His face was pale. Richard leaned toward him. "Titus, are you alright?" Titus shook his head.

"I need some air," he whispered, stepping out from the group. Richard followed him.

"Titus, you can't run from God. It doesn't do any good." Titus walked a little farther before turning around to face Richard.

"Not now, Mason. I can't do it. Not today."

"Please, Titus, don't reject it any longer. Today is the day of salvation. You may not have another chance. Please, Titus-"

"Go away, Mason! I need to think. Maybe later on, but not now. Leave me alone." He turned and practically ran to his tent.

Richard looked down and shook his head. *Lord, please get a hold of his heart before it's too late,* he prayed.

169

He returned to the "church" and stood in the back during the closing prayer. Some soldiers left after the prayer, but many stayed and thanked the Chaplain for the message. It took Richard forever to get back to the front with the others. By the time he reached them, the crowd was dispersing and Isaac had told Seth about Richard going after Titus.

Seth looked hopeful. He was very concerned for the soldier's soul. When Richard told him what Titus had said, he shook his head. "We just have to keep praying," Seth said firmly. "We can't give up on him."

★1861★

Chapter 20

★

A Land of Cotton...And More Cotton

Therefore I say unto you, What things soever ye desire, when ye
pray, believe that ye receive them, and ye shall have them.
Mark 11:24

The Masons began cotton harvest in September. Silas had hired several men from neighboring communities to help out, along with the family.

Some of the Naces helped on and off as they had time. Josiah Lanier, an apprentice, was a hard worker. Not one word of complaint was heard from him.

Michael swatted at a mosquito on his arm. They were coming from the creek back of the Masons' large property.

Carter paused from his work to straighten out his back. As he did, he saw a long line of Confederate soldiers marching Northward out of town. The others followed Carter's gaze and stopped their work to wave and shout, "Goodbye and God bless!"

The soldiers smiled and waved back. The fifer played a rousing patriotic tune.

Among the group of soldiers was Joel Lanier. Josiah's eyes locked on his brother. He waved and Joel waved back. "Bye, Joel! God bless!"

Silas placed a hand on Josiah's shoulder. "Do you want to run tell him goodbye?"

Josiah shook his head. "I'm not gonna drag it out. We said goodbye at the pond this morning. It was special, just me and him. I'm gonna miss him."

Michael readjusted his work gloves and started picking cotton again. As far as he was concerned, this was the easy part. He had to admit, he didn't much care for the upcoming seeding process.

★ 1861 ★

Later that day, Michael went to his room to rest his aching back. As he entered the room, he saw Richard and Seth's latest letter lying on his bed. With a smile, he picked it up and lay down to read it again.

Dear Dixie and Michael,

Hey! How are y'all? We're doing great. Jordan and Isaac said to tell you Hey. Not too much action around here except drilling and such. Well, I take that back. We did have a little excitement on the 21st of August. Some Yanks drove the picket line out of their jurisdiction, but we soon reclaimed our position, as the Yankees didn't intend a real attack. They were beyond Fairfax Court House before all was said and done. But nothing's been going on since then. We're thankful for this time of peace. Many say it is short lived, but we might as well enjoy it while we can!

General Jackson is quite a man! He is praying man. He often goes out to secluded places in the woods to pray. We're glad to serve under such a Godly man.

But there is something a bit...well, strange about General Jackson. (To be honest there are a good many 'different' things about him.) He likes to suck on lemons as if they were candy! And he is rather secretive concerning military orders. But at least we don't have to worry about the Yankees learning of his plans!

He certainly seems to enjoy marching us about. If it is like this in time of peace, I can't imagine how it will be in war time. But then perhaps we will be used to it by then!

School's back in, right? Work hard and get good grades, Michael. It's hard to believe you're in seventh grade already! It won't be long 'till you're graduating! And Dixie, hope you have an uneventful year of teaching. Remember, how you teach them now will affect their futures. We're praying for you!

Cotton time's just around the corner. Too bad we can't help with the harvest this year. We were talking the other day about how we actually missed cotton harvest! Well, not exactly miss it, but anything that would mean this war was over and we were home with y'all sounds wonderful right now!

Oh! Come to think of it we did have a small bit of excitement the other night! Remember Jeremy Calling? Well, he was on guard duty and was getting kinda sleepy. He started dozing and was startled awake by someone walking through the camp.

He shouted for the person to halt, but instead, it took off running. So Jeremy fired his gun. This woke the whole camp up and everyone came running to see what happened. Come to find out, a deer had wandered into the camp. That's what Jeremy had heard. He wounded it and had to finish it off, and we had deer meat to add to our rations!

We finally received our official supplies from Richmond. We received a "sack coat" which simply means we don't have those long coats the officers wear. Ours are Cadet gray and are pretty warm, though I'm not sure how long they'll stay that way. They ain't the best quality. They also sent us kepis, but we prefer our slouch hats. They provide more cover when it rains and protection from the sun too.

We each got a knapsack, bayonet scabbards and haversacks. The rest was regulation uniform items not important enough to mention. We already had our blankets, canteens, cups and little things like that. So I guess now we are "real" soldiers!

Nothing else really interesting to write about, things have been so quiet. Got to get this in the mail before it leaves.

We love and miss y'all.
Richard and Seth

★1861★

Tyler glanced around the group that had gathered in front of him. This was the start of a weekly prayer meeting which was Chaplain Matthews' idea. And those who helped organize the meeting had voted to make Tyler the leader. He was nervous.

The only reason he'd agreed to do it was because he felt it was a good opportunity to serve his Savior.

"Well, I guess we should get this started. We have two main prayer requests to let y'all know about. The first is for the salvation of Titus Mallory, one of our fellow soldiers. I'm not sure who all knows him, but he really needs the Lord."

Tyler cleared his throat and continued. "The second is for his brother, Jim. He's in jail on false charges of treason. Titus is very upset about this, and he thinks if God cared He would get Jim out of this. This is one thing that's holding him back from Salvation. Please make these a fervent matter of prayer. Umm...does anyone else have a request on their heart this evening?"

Other requests were made known. "Well, I suppose we should pray now. Umm, I guess I'll start and y'all can join in or just pray silently." Seth grinned. Tyler was so nervous!

"Heavenly Father, we come before You now with many requests on our hearts," Tyler began slowly. "Thank You for the blessings You've brought our way, and we ask for Thy continued blessings upon us. Lord, please lay heavy conviction on the heart of Titus Mallory until he comes to know You as his Savior. Please convict his heart of his lost condition.

"And Lord, please be with Jim Mallory right now. Please let the authorities see through the lies his prosecutors have charged him with. Give him strength to go through this trial. Let him feel Your presence with him, and may he be like Paul and Silas in the Bible, who were able to praise You while under harsh treatment. Let justice prevail and Your name be glorified..."

The other soldiers began to pray aloud, begging God to work a miracle in the Mallory family. Seth glanced up at his friend in surprise to make sure it really was Tyler leading in prayer. He'd never heard Tyler pray with such power in front of anyone. He really seemed at full liberty. Seth grinned and continued praying.

Unawares to the group, Titus had walked up during the prayer meeting. He heard his name and his brother's called out.

He rolled his eyes. *Won't do any good,* he thought. *God don't hear prayers for my family.*

★ 1861 ★

"I can't believe the kittens are two months old!" exclaimed Lana as she picked up the fluffy tortoiseshell kitten. The kitten's sandpapery tongue licked at Lana's fingers. "Are you gonna keep any of them?" Lana asked.

"We're keeping Bandit," Dixie affirmed, stroking the black and white kitten, "but we're giving away the rest. Since we already have Peek-a-boo and Old Tom, Mama says three cats are enough. Do you want one?"

Lana grinned sheepishly. "Papa said if y'all were giving them away, I could get a couple. We have a mouse problem in the barn."

Dixie smiled. "Go ahead and pick them out. They're old enough now."

Lana smiled. "I can't resist this tortoiseshell. She's so sweet! I'll take her. And I think that other black and white one will be my second choice." The kittens purred contentedly as the girls descended from the loft. Dixie waved goodbye as Lana walked home.

"Dixie!" Michael called. "Mama's got some cotton for us to seed. We can do it in the barn. By the way, Annie and Carter are stopping by in a little while to get a couple kittens."

Dixie nodded. "Let's see how much we can get seeded before they get here. Lana just left with two."

Soon baskets of cotton surrounded the children. As Dixie turned the crank on the gin to seed the fluffy cotton, she thought over the first verse of '*Dixieland*' once again. Michael fed the cotton into the machine and made sure nothing jammed.

"I must say, I completely agree," she said out of the blue.

"You agree with what?" Michael asked. Dixie had a habit of making comments, forgetting others didn't know what she was thinking about.

"The South is definitely *the land of cotton*! When we go up North, and I see how they run things, I wish I was in the 'Land of Cotton.' When we toured that factory a few years back, it made me appreciate working cotton. I ought to be more thankful that I have the opportunity to work. I'm sorry I haven't been a better example."

Michael kept feeding in the cotton. "It's alright, Dixie. I haven't had the best attitude either. We can both do better with God's help."

"Hello? Anyone here?" Carter and Annie stepped in with Alyssa Rose. "We're here to get two kittens," Carter continued.

As if on cue, the kittens came racing out of the barn loft. Ever the showoff, Cowboy, who was in the lead, jumped into the air as he ran, landing in a pile of cotton.

The young people laughed as the kitten franticly tried to free himself. Finally he was able to waddle out of his cotton prison.

"There's my Cowboy!" exclaimed Alyssa Rose, as she picked up the skinny gray kitten. Alyssa Rose had given him his nickname before. She looked at Annie with pleading eyes.

"We'll get Cowboy, Lissy. I like him too. Carter, you can pick the other."

Carter looked over the kittens. A white kitten with a calico stripe down her back caught his attention. Michael grinned as Carter picked her up. The little fluff ball wriggled a little, but soon relaxed and leaned into Carter. He cast a glance at Michael. "We're gonna call her Sumter. No girly names will work for me!" The two boys laughed.

"I guess we'd better be getting home. Mama wanted us to get right back. Thank y'all so much!" said Annie.

"No thanks necessary, Annie. Y'all are doing us a favor by taking them," Dixie replied.

★ 1861 ★

"Calling!" Jeremy eagerly stepped forward to receive his letter. He hadn't heard from home in a long time. He smiled as he recognized his sister Cornelia's handwriting. Jeremy opened the letter as he thought of his sixteen year old sister. They were only sixteen months apart in age and had always been pretty close.

He hurried to his tent to read his letter. Titus and Alvin Willis were already there and barely glanced up as Jeremy laid on his pallet to read the coveted note.

Dear Jeremiah,

I am sorry this letter is so long in coming! Things have been quite busy, for Father's work closed their North Carolina branch and we have moved to the Massachusetts' branch. Here is our new address…

Jeremy wasn't surprised that his family had moved without telling him. He often had to happen upon information to know anything that was going on. He squinted to read the next paragraph; it was terribly watermarked.

I've been elected bearer of what to you may be bad news, but for the family is a great honor. I don't know how to tell you, as I, for one, don't see any cause for jubilation. The fact of the matter is that our brother, Darrell, has been offered and has accepted a commission in the United States Army as a Lieutenant…

Chapter 21

★

Letters

...And there is a friend that sticketh closer than a brother.
Proverbs 18:24b

Jeremy felt as if he'd been punched in the stomach. "What?" he exclaimed out loud. Alvin looked up at Jeremy's stricken face. He almost asked what was wrong, but he knew Jeremy wouldn't notice; he was still absorbed in the letter.

> *Jeremiah, please understand that I fully agree with the Union. But I do believe that it is wrong for family to fight against each other. Darrell shouldn't have accepted the commission until you returned home. You will return when your enlistment is up won't you? You must! Our family cannot be divided like this nation is.*
>
> *Why did you have to join the Confederacy anyway? Jeremiah, you're not the rebel type. Please come home. I miss you so much. Father says if you'll come home after your enlistment is up (he thinks it would*

179

be wrong for you to desert), you are welcome to come
to Massachusetts. But...

Here the ink was smudged, crossed out and the sentence restarted.

But if you will not leave the rebellion, Father said
you may not return. He said he didn't fully
understand the gravity of the situation when he
allowed you to go, but being aware now, he regrets
granting you permission. If you remain, you no
longer have his blessing.

Oh, Jeremiah, come home!...

Jeremy felt sick. He laid the letter aside. He couldn't read anymore, not now. He thought of his family. In all, there were seven children in the Calling family. Jeremy loved and missed his brothers and sisters. Why did differences have to tear them apart?

Why has Darrell gone and joined the Union? he wondered. *What should I do?*

Alvin looked at his friend. "What's wrong, Jeremy? Is the world coming to an end?"

"My world is," came the subdued reply. "My family has moved to Massachusetts and my older brother's joined the Yankee army. My sister's begging me to come home when my enlistment is up."

The other soldiers were paying attention now. Titus spoke up with a disgusted, sarcastic tone, "Nice family you got there, Jeremy."

"Titus," Alvin scolded. "Not now."

Jeremy was struggling with his feelings. Anger welled up inside him. The news had really hurt. How dare they move without telling him! Why couldn't things be different with his family? Why would parents, much less Christian ones, act like this?

He immediately felt the Holy Spirit smite his heart. He shouldn't even entertain such thoughts, especially anger towards his parents! A silent prayer of repentance helped to stop the thoughts. But his heart still ached for his family to be reconciled.

"I don't know how to answer this letter," he sighed.

Alvin shrugged. "Whatever you decide, you'd better wait until you've really thought it out." Jeremy nodded in agreement.

"I need some air," Jeremy said suddenly, tossing the letter onto his pallet and walking outside.

Alvin glanced down at the letter. "Hmm…Springfield, Massachusetts…"

★ 1861 ★

"Goodbye, Mrs. Armistead. Enjoy your kittens," Dixie called. Mrs. Armistead said goodbye and hurried down the road.

Michael, who was returning from town, greeted Mrs. Armistead as she passed him. He hurried up to Dixie. "Great! That's all of them!"

Dixie grinned. "I know! Oh, you have the mail! Anything for me?"

Michael grinned slyly. "Well aren't we curious? You'll just have to wait and see!" With that, he took off for the house with Dixie trailing not far behind. Michael darted in the front door and raced to the kitchen. Dixie was in hot pursuit, reaching the kitchen as Michael triumphantly handed the mail to Papa. Mama and Mrs. Bradley laughed as Dixie panted in.

Papa chuckled as he sorted the mail. "Oh, Dixie, you have a letter from Matilda Tanner. Here you go."

"Thanks! She hasn't written since July!" Dixie took the letter and smiled satisfactorily at Michael. He returned the look, holding up a letter from their cousin Bruce Culwright.

"Did the boys write?" Mama inquired.

"Not this time. But they'll send one before too long, I'm sure. And it will be addressed to the most beautiful woman on earth."

Mrs. Bradley laughed as Mama blushed. "Silas, not in front of the children!" she said with a smile.

"Well, it's the truth, isn't it children?"

All voiced their agreement. Mama just shook her head and turned to see if Mrs. Bradley needed any more help in the kitchen. Papa and the children grinned at each other.

It was now October 3rd. Many things had happened in the last months, as far as war news.

On the 29th of August, Maj. General Benjamin Butler[15] led an unfortunately successful attack on Hatteras Inlet, North Carolina. The next day, Gen. John Frémont[16] proclaimed martial law in Missouri and then ordered the confiscation of property from Missourians aiding the Confederacy.

The Masons were concerned for Silas' younger brother, Wesley and his family who lived in Missouri. So far, they hadn't heard anything from them concerning their property.

September 4th, Confederate Maj. General Leonidas Polk[17] took Columbus, Kentucky, which ended Kentucky's neutrality. On the 6th, Ulysses S. Grant[18], a Union Brig. General, and his troops took Paducah, Kentucky.

The 10th of September, General Albert Sidney Johnston[19] was given command of the Confederate armies of the west. Maj. General Sterling Price[20] and his troops captured the Union garrison at Lexington, Missouri on the 20th.

---

[15] He will later become famous when he and his army take and occupy New Orleans (May-December 1862).

[16] Frémont will later be nominated for President against Lincoln in 1864, but will withdraw later that year.

[17] Close friend of President Jefferson Davis. Polk will serve chiefly in the western and deep southern states.

[18] Grant will go on to play a chief part in the Battle of Shiloh in 1862.

[19] Commander of the Western armies. Johnston's great day will come in April of 1862.

[20] Price has a strong desire to see his native state of Missouri join the Confederacy, which he will attempt to bring about throughout the war.

Dixie soon realized that before the war was over, she was going to need another blank book to hold her news articles. She was thankful for the articles she received from other family members and from out of town newspapers as well as their town newspaper.

Dixie sat down on her bed to read her letter. How she missed her friend. The Tanners had moved to Delaware back in April. Mrs. Tanner and the younger children used to sit on the pew across from the Masons at church, but Mr. Tanner and Matilda's older brother Brandon never came to church.

She glanced over her bed and noticed she had left her teaching books scattered all over. Putting them away, she sat back down to read.

> *...Oh, Dixie, I don't know what to do! Brandon has joined the Delaware infantry. He's so full of wrath toward the Confederates. He said, "Those Rebels are going to get it when Delaware starts fighting them. We will have them begging to join the Union again. You just wait and see!"*
>
> *Papa has joined too and is already a Captain! I think they rush things so! Mama cries all the time now. I fear I cannot write more, I am too upset and broken over this.*
>
> *Tearfully yours,*
> *Matilda Tanner*

Dixie read the letter in horror. Could anything possibly be worse? She flew down the stairs and read the letter aloud to her family. They immediately began to pray for the Tanners.

When they finished, Papa took the letter. "I believe Pastor Brewster needs to know about this. He's expressed concern for the Tanners lately. I'll be back later."

 ★ 1861 ★

Chapter 22

★

Sharp Encounter

But whoso shall offend one of these little ones which believe in me, it were better for him that a millstone were hanged about his neck, and that he were drowned in the depth of the sea.
Matthew 18:6

" . . . Give me Liberty, or GIVE ME DEATH!" The classroom erupted in applause. Martha Alistair had just recited Patrick Henry's famous speech.

"Very well presented, Martha! Your recitation has earned you a 100% grade!" Lana praised. The class clapped once again as Martha took her seat.

Just at that moment, Sheriff Gallimore came to the back door. "Miss Brewster, may I have a word with you?" he asked politely. Her father stood nearby, looking grim.

"Class, please start with your readers," Lana instructed. She stepped out with her father and the sheriff. The door was left ajar, and Dixie turned back to helping a first grader with a new word.

Suddenly, Sheriff Gallimore's voice rose slightly and Dixie's ear caught a phrase that made her heart skip a beat: "...Union soldiers camped on Running Deer Green."

No! She thought. *This can't be happening! That's less than two miles from my house! No!*

At that moment, Lana reentered and calmly told the children, "Class dismissed." For a moment, no one moved. It was only 11:45! Then one at a time the children filed out. To their surprise, their parents were waiting for them.

Michael whispered to his mother, "What's going on?"

"We'll explain when we get home," was her reply. The Masons hurried home. Dixie noticed they took the long way home, so as not to pass Running Deer Green.

It was late October, and all these precautions made Dixie even more nervous. Then she remembered: the Williams family lived on Running Deer Green! Would the Yankees run them off if they found out their son was in the Confederate army? The thought made her tremble. None of their girls had shown up at school that day. Surely the Yankees wouldn't massacre them!

The Masons hurried inside. Dixie took off her wraps and shoes and headed to the parlor with the others. She stopped in the doorway. There was the Williams family, safe and sound!

Dixie's words tumbled out quickly. "How long have y'all been here? Is everyone alight? What happened?"

Marianna smiled at her niece. "We've been here for about three hours. As for what happened, we will tell when everyone has gotten settled."

Everyone quickly found a seat in the parlor, and Mrs. Bradley brought in some coffee. Uncle Dean began the story. "We were eating breakfast when we thought we heard horses and gunshots in the distance. We thought nothing of it, because lots of people hunt out our way.

"We heard a shout just as the girls were leaving for school. I glanced out the window and saw some Federals up the hill. I called the girls back inside. We weren't sure if they were going to raid the house or not, so we started hiding valuables in a concealed place. Marianna started packing some clothes for the girls just in case they should order us out.

"Then we heard some loud pounding on the front door and someone shouted, 'Open up! This is the United States Army. Open up!'"

Dixie trembled, while Michael leaned forward to catch every word. "I told the others to stay upstairs, and I headed down. When I opened the door, I saw about twenty-five Yankees standing in my front yard."

Uncle Dean smiled as Dixie cringed. Imagine! Twenty-five Yankees! "They told me I had five minutes to clear the premises. I said, 'I'm sorry, young man, but you've forgotten something very important. North Carolina isn't part of the Union anymore.'"

Dixie gasped. She knew that would set the Yankees off. And Uncle Dean confirmed that the Yank looked as angry as a hornet. "As it turns out, my words didn't mean much to him. We gathered our things, saddled the horses, and came here. The neighbors are watching the house and promised to let us know when the Yankees leave."

It was arranged that the Williams would stay with the Masons. The girls liked the idea of camping out in Dixie's room and the guest room was given to Uncle Dean and Aunt Marianna. As they fell asleep that night, Dixie couldn't help but wonder why the Yankees were in Four Tree Springs.

★ 1861 ★

The next day, Michael was bagging up some cotton for Mrs. Bradley to spin into thread later. There was a knock at the door, so he rose to answer it. "Yes, may I help-oh!" There in front of him was a Confederate soldier!

"Excuse me, young man, but is your Pa at home?"

"Y-yes, sir. Please, come in and have a seat while I get him." Michael hurried up the stairs to his father's office.

"Papa! There's a soldier down stairs to see you!"

"Oh? Is he one of our soldiers?"

"Yes, Papa." Silas quickly followed his son down the stairs. The young man stood as they entered the room.

Before Mr. Mason could say anything, the soldier crossed the room, shook hands with him and said, "I'm Joseph Richardson, North Carolina volunteer. You must be Mr. Silas Mason."

"Yes, I'm Silas Mason. Pardon my asking, but how do you know who I am?"

Joseph's eyes twinkled. "Word gets around." In a more serious tone, he said, "I need to ask a favor of you, Mr. Mason."

Sensing that they may need to talk privately, Michael looked at his father and said, "Excuse me; I'll go upstairs"

"Oh, I didn't mean for you to leave," Joseph said quickly. "I'm sorry if I alarmed you."

"Oh, you didn't. I just thought you two would rather talk alone." He took a step toward the staircase.

"Michael, you may stay," Silas invited, knowing he did want to know about the strange favor, but not wanting to be rude. Michael didn't hesitate and came back and stood next to his father. "Besides," Papa added, "I think I can trust you not to go down to Running Deer Green and report what you hear!"

Michael laughed. "No worries about that, Papa!"

Joseph nodded. "So you know about our unwelcome guests. That's what I'm here about." The three sat down and Joseph lowered his voice. "Some friends of mine and I have been keeping an eye on this group of Yankees. We need a campsite closer to the Yankee encampment. We'd like to camp on your land back by the creek."

"Of course, y'all can stay there, by all means. Let us know if there's anything y'all need."

Joseph thanked Silas for his cooperation. He informed them that his commander, Captain Beasley, was a fellow North Carolinian. "If for any reason you need to get in contact with us, just tell them who you are and ask for me or Captain Beasley."

"We will. Joseph, may I pray with you before you leave?"

Joseph's face lit up. "Yes, I would like that!" Silas prayed for Joseph's protection and blessings on the camp's operations. When he finished, Joseph said, "Thank you so much, Mr. Mason."

"You're welcome, Joseph." They shook hands, and Silas showed him out. Michael hurried to finish bagging the cotton. Never in his life had he worked so fast. The very thought of Confederate scouts staying on their property spurred him on. How exciting!

★ 1861 ★

Later that day, Ellen sent Dixie and Michael to town for some things. After telling them to take the long way, she let them go. "Just stay away from the soldiers as much as possible," she cautioned.

When they got to town, there wasn't a bluecoat in sight. In fact, there was no one around at all. They made most of their purchases at the general store. They had a couple other stops before they could head home.

Michael offered to stay outside with the packages at the last stop. Since there were no Yankees around, Dixie agreed and stepped into the store. Michael admired the iron benches on the store porch. The intricate designs amazed him. He admired the sharply wrought edges and wondered if one day he could make something like that.

"Hey, you!" Michael jerked his head up in surprise. His heart sank. Standing near the porch were five Union soldiers. Remembering his mother's warning to stay away from the Yanks, he picked up the packages he had laid on the bench earlier and attempted to go inside the store.

"Wait just a minute, little guy. Where do you think you are going?" asked one rather tall and strongly built soldier, who seemed to be the leader. He was standing on the steps leading up to the building.

Michael replied, "Inside." He wasn't about to waste any breath on lengthy explanations. He turned toward the door.

"So sorry," the Yank said, coming to stand between Michael and the door, "but you have to stay out here and answer some questions." The Yankee took a step toward Michael.

"I'm not allowed to talk to strangers, sir."

"Well, I can fix that. I'm Pvt. Badin. Now I'm not a stranger."

Michael swallowed hard. "Sir, I need to go inside."

The Yank grinned slyly. "Not so fast. Aren't children supposed to obey their elders? I think I'm a bit older than you, kid, so if I say you stay out, you stay out!"

"Yeah, Rodney, you show him who's in charge!" one of the other soldiers called.

Beads of sweat began to appear on the boy's forehead. This guy was starting to scare him. "Sorry. Don't have time."

"Well, you better make time. What's your name?"

Michael took a deep breath. "Sir, I told you I'm not allowed to talk to strangers. Please, just let me go inside."

Rodney took another menacing step toward Michael. "What's this?" he said, taking one of Michael's packages. He proceeded to tear off the wrapping. Michael started to protest, but thought better of it.

"Hmm…salt huh? Looks like this packaging would bust real easy," he said. He threw it down on the bench. The package hit hard and began to spill onto the porch. Michael looked at the salt pouring out.

The soldier grabbed him by the shoulders and jerked him around. "As I recall, I asked you what your name was. You haven't answered me yet."

Michael was very scared now. He knew all five Yanks were carrying pistols, and although he didn't think they would shoot a child, he wasn't intending to find out. *Dear Lord,* he prayed silently, *please protect me! I don't know what this Yankee is about, but he's scaring me. Please send someone to help!*

The Yankee was mere inches from Michael's face. "You better start talking, Little Reb." He lifted Michael off his feet by his shirt collar.

"P-please, sir, I don't want trouble!" Michael sputtered.

One of the other soldiers jeered, "Oh, come on, Badin. Let the kid down. He isn't hurting anything."

"Sure thing." He turned loose of Michael, and pushed him backwards as he fell to the ground. His head immediately made contact with the sharp edge of the iron bench.

"OH! OUCH!" Michael tried to stand up, but he was too dizzy. He held his head and laid all the way down on the porch. He bit his lip to keep from hollering, but he couldn't hold it all back. He couldn't think straight.

At that moment Dixie and Mr. and Mrs. Wheeling, who owned the store, came out of the back room. As Dixie made her purchase, some movement outside caught her eye. She gasped when she saw, through the large store window, the Yankee shouting at something on the ground out of her sight.

"Where's Michael?"

Mrs. Wheeling looked up. "Was he with you?"

"Yes, he's supposed to be waiting for me on the porch."

With that said, Mr. Wheeling headed for the door.

The Yankee looked down at Michael. He hadn't intended to hurt the kid, just scare him. And the longer the kid lay there, the more of a chance there was that somebody would walk by. "Get up, little Rebel. You aren't hurt."

The door swung open. "What's going on here?" bellowed Mr. Wheeling. The soldier looked up at the tall man. Dixie hurried to her younger brother's side.

"Well…um…you see, um…" Rodney stammered.

"Out with it, boy!"

Before he could respond, a Union sergeant rode up to the shop. "Privates, you are to report to Lieutenant Dodson right away."

"Yes, sir." The soldiers left, and Dixie recognized the sergeant. It took her a moment to remember where she'd seen him before. He was the soldier who had come to Four Tree Springs in April. He had nearly run over Martha Alistair and had stopped to make sure she was alright. They had also seen him at the horse sale.

Sgt. Evans looked at Michael. The boy's eyes reflected his pain. He didn't need an explanation. He had a good idea what had happened.

Dixie helped Michael sit up. "Oh! Michael, you're bleeding." He pulled his handkerchief out of his pocket and Dixie used it to slow the bleeding. "What happened?"

Michael tried to tell her, but his head ached too much.

"There is no way he can walk home like that. Why don't I take you two home?" Sgt. Evans offered.

Mr. Wheeling objected. "That won't be necessary. I'll drive them home."

Sgt. Evans nodded. "May I follow you, sir? I don't mean to intrude on personal business, but if one of my men were involved, I need to be sure and report this."

"Come along then."

Before long, the children were home. Dixie hopped out of the wagon. Mr. Wheeling helped Michael out of the wagon and into the house. Ellen and Aunt Marianna were chatting in the sitting room. Ellen gasped when she saw Michael.

Michael was led to the sofa and Aunt Marianna hurried to get some cold water and a rag to place on the gash. Michael finally managed to tell his mother and Sgt. Evans what had happened. Ellen's face was flushed with indignation. "How could anyone be so cruel to a child?"

Sgt. Evans was furious. "I assure you, Ma'am, I will see to it that the soldier responsible will be reprimanded for this." Calming down somewhat, he asked Michael for a description of the soldier who had hurt him. Michael told what he could and mentioned the name Badin.

The sergeant nodded. "I should have known. Ma'am, is there anything I can do to help?"

"No, thank you. You've helped us enough," replied Ellen, hugging her son.

Sgt. Evans nodded and soon left.

Michael's head ached so badly that he couldn't stop a moan from escaping his lips. "Poor child," murmured Mama. "Do you want to lie down, son?"

"Yes, ma'am. I'm sorry about the salt. I forgot to tell Dixie to get some more."

Dixie and Mama looked at each other. Aunt Marianna said, "He's this hurt, and he's worried about salt? Ellen, I'm telling you, he's just like his father! Silas was just like that when he was still at home! Seems like the apple didn't fall too far from the tree."

Mama squeezed Michael's shoulder. "Michael, don't worry about the salt. I'll get some bandages. Dixie, hold this rag in place for me."

"Yes, ma'am."

Mama returned and bandaged Michael's cut. She shook her head. "From now on, I think Papa needs to get the groceries. I'll not risk this happening again."

★ 1861 ★

October 26th dawned bright yet chilly outside. Mr. Bradley tended the kitchen fire while Silas started one in the sitting room. Dixie shivered as she hurried down the stairs. The other girls followed her.

Michael brought up the rear. His head still ached, but he was doing much better. Sgt. Evans was true to his word and justice had been done. The soldier had been punished and was made to apologize.

Aunt Marianna looked up from some mending as the children entered the sitting room. "Look at that, Ellen. The girls match!" Each girl was wearing a caramel colored dress. They had made the discovery that morning that they each had one and decided to wear them.

"Well, these girls look all set for some excitement," Uncle Dean teased. The girls giggled.

"So sorry to disappoint you, Uncle Dean, but I think it's just going to be another Saturday," Dixie said, mocking a sigh as they all headed for the dining room.

As they finished breakfast, they heard a light knock at the back door. Mr. Bradley left the room to answer it. He opened the door. "Yes?"

A couple, who looked to be in their mid-thirties, stood on the porch. Two boys and a girl stood behind them, and the lady looked like she was expecting. The dark skinned man said, "Pardon, Suh. I'm Will and dis be my wife Lou and our young'uns. We be lookin' for some work. We just come from Maryland and we's hard workers. "

Chapter 23
★
Race Against Time

Therefore to him that knoweth to do good, and doeth it not, to him it is sin.
James 4:17

M r. Bradley was surprised but knew Silas would want to talk to them. Silas was called for and offered a warm handshake to the newcomers. After Mr. Bradley explained why they were there, Silas said, "I'd like to talk to you. I may be able to use your help, sir. Let's step into my office."

Will and Lou looked at him in surprise. "You really want us to come inside, suh? All of us?"

"Of course, if you don't mind. My wife will take your wife and the children to the sitting room. They'll be just fine." With that said, they headed inside.

The family was surprised by the sudden arrival of the guests, but delighted when they discovered that they wanted to help out around the plantation. Dixie, Michael and the Williams girls joined Ellen in the sitting room to help entertain the little ones.

Dixie learned the children's names were Reuben, Salina May and Troy. Troy was near Michael and looked at his bandaged head curiously. "What happened?"

"Troy, mind your place," Mrs. Roberts said softly.

Michael smiled. "It's fine, Mrs. Roberts. I gashed it on an iron bench in town. It's healing up though."

Troy looked at Michael in surprise. "How'd you do dat?"

"Troy!" Mrs. Roberts scolded.

Ellen was rather amused. "Michael had a little run in with a bully in town. But everything's been taken care of with that."

Mrs. Roberts looked sternly at Troy. "You need to quit being so nosey, young'un!"

"Sorry, Mama."

Mrs. Roberts nodded.

Meanwhile in the office the men were discussing business. Silas asked Will where they were from. "I was reared in Maryland and Lou, she's from everywhere. Maryland, California, New York, Virginia, she's lived all over before we got married."

"Where are y'all staying now?" Silas asked.

"In a wagon, basically. I'm tryin' to find a job, den we'll try to find a house to rent. I'm hoping for something permanent in dis area. Everyone's been kind to us here, even if dey didn't need hired help."

Silas was thinking of the old Morris place. It was small, but nice and wouldn't cost much to rent it. Better yet, it was nestled on a parcel of land right next to the south field.

"Well, Mr. Roberts, I'm very interested in hiring you. Two of my sons went off to war and I'm a little short of hands this year. I need to know, are you a free man? 'Cause we don't want any trouble here at Shady Grove."

Mr. Roberts smiled. "Yes, suh. I's got papers for my whole family. Worked hard for 'em too."

"Good, good. It would be nice to have permanent help. I can't afford a large salary for you, but it will be enough to live off of, and if you do stay on with me, in the harvest months, you'll get part of our food crops for your family as payment."

Mr. Roberts nodded. "I am interested, suh, but I have to ask. What army is your sons serving in?"

"Confederate."

Mr. Roberts grinned broadly. "It's a deal Mr. Mason, suh."

Silas and Will went to town and returned at dinner with good news: the Morris house was now being rented to the Roberts family.

★ 1861 ★

A few days later Michael was heading home from school. The Yankees hadn't caused any trouble lately, and school had reopened. Dixie wasn't teaching that day and the Williams cousins had gone on ahead with the Nace girls, so Michael's only companion was Confederate. Tied to the saddle horn was a bag of onions that Lana had sent with him to deliver to Widow Lanier.

As he rode past the bank, the bag of onions came untied, and the onions rolled into the alley. Sighing, Michael dismounted and began picking up the onions. He turned to leave but stopped when he heard hushed voices at the other end of the alley, behind the bank.

"I knew those Rebels were trailing us!" someone said in a loud, disgusted voice. Michael froze. Usually, he wouldn't eavesdrop, but something told him this time, he should. He edged closer to the voices.

Michael detected three separate voices, but only one sounded familiar. Scooting closer, he ducked behind some crates. From where he hid, he could see all of them. He recognized Rodney Badin, the soldier who had caused all the trouble at the store. Michael inadvertently reached back and touched his head, shuddering at the memory of the recent wound.

His heart seemed to beat so loud that he feared it was audible. He knew that if he was caught, it wouldn't be a pleasant situation. He pushed that thought away. *Dear Lord, please keep me safe,* he prayed silently.

The other man was dressed as a sergeant. He spoke next, "Capt. Badin, I am of a mind to rush them. We have the numbers to do it and according to our scouts, there are only a few of them. They are camping out about two and a half miles from our camp on that big plantation. We could wipe them out before anyone would know what happened."

Michael cringed. They were talking about Capt. Beasley's group, alright. He listened as they laid out their plans. Then Capt. Badin said, "Murdock, you are a genius! You and Rodney head back to camp and put our plans in action. I'll meet you there in thirty minutes, and we'll attack in forty-five. Hurry! Don't let this leak out. I don't want the Rebels to find out."

They dispersed and Michael rushed back to Confederate. He tossed the onions into his saddle bag and lit out for home. *We've got to warn them! We've got to! Oh, Dear Lord, please help us get to the camp before it's too late!*

He knew his father, Uncle Dean, and the workers were all in the east field so he headed there. Silas looked up as Michael and Confederate thundered onto the field. The boy started talking before he'd even stopped. His words tumbled out so fast, no one could understand him.

"Michael, slow down, son. I can't get a word you're saying. Son, calm down!" Papa said, half amused, half concerned; Michael sounded on the verge of panic.

"Papa! Yankees! They're gonna try to crush Capt. Beasley's men! We gotta warn them! I heard them talking!" Michael quickly filled his father in on the details.

Papa turned to Uncle Dean. "I'm going with Michael to the camp. Dean, pray!" He quickly swung up in front of Michael onto Confederate, and the two took off.

Every minute seemed like an hour. They didn't have much time to reach the camp. Michael hoped there would be enough time for an escape. Confederate ran for all he was worth.

Finally, the camp came into view. They splashed across the creek and brought Confederate to an abrupt stop. He gave a few small, excited bucks as Michael and Silas slid off. Joseph Richardson grasped Confederate's bridle and calmed him down. Scouts seemed to appear from everywhere.

"We need to see Capt. Beasley," Silas announced.

"What's going on here?" a man in an officer's uniform demanded. "I'm Capt. Beasley." His voice sounded stern, but he seemed to wear a constant smile. Michael liked him right away.

"My son stumbled upon some Yankees planning to attack your unit, sir." He glanced at his pocket watch. "According to what he heard, they attack in twenty minutes."

The Captain looked concerned. He turned to Michael. "How did you come by this information, son?"

Michael quickly replied. "I dropped some onions in an alley and when I went to pick them up, I heard them talking. They said they knew y'all were following them, and they said they wanted to crush your unit."

"Son, we have to know you're telling the truth," Capt. Beasley said. Some of the soldiers had begun packing up their saddlebags, just in case. "Can you prove your story is true?"

Michael shrugged. "The onions are in my saddle bag with my schoolbooks. Does that help?"

"He's telling the truth," one scout affirmed, holding up an onion, removed from the bag.

Joseph pushed through the group of soldiers surrounding the Masons. "Captain, these are the people who are letting us stay here. They're for us."

Before Capt. Beasley could make a reply, a scout raced into the camp, panting hard. "Capt. Beasley, beg to report."

"Report, sir."

"The Yanks are forming a marching formation. They're heading this way!"

"Strike the tent! We leave immediately!" The camp burst into activity. Before long, Michael couldn't tell the camp had been there at all.

Captain Beasley shook hands with Silas and Michael. "Thank you for your help, sirs. We are greatly in your debt."

"God speed," Silas said, as he and Michael remounted and rode back towards home.

★ 1861 ★

"Michael Mason! Tell me you're teasing!" Dixie stared at her brother in disbelief. Everyone had gathered at Grandpa and Grandma's and were in a state of shocked astonishment.

"No, I'm not. I didn't do it alone, though. God's the one who reminded me that Papa was in the east field. If it hadn't been for Papa, I wouldn't have known what to do." Michael was still trembling. The adrenaline was gone now, leaving him as weak as a dish rag. He was sitting between his parents in his grandparent's sitting room.

Mama put her arm around Michael. Papa smiled at his son and said, "I'm proud of you, Buddy. God helped us get there in time for them to escape. I believe God let you overhear their plans on purpose. One thing we know, He made sure your bag wasn't tied well!" Everyone laughed.

A few days later, the joyous news that the Yankees were gone for good reached Four Tree Springs. The Williams moved back into their ransacked house. But to their relief the things they had hidden had been undisturbed. Everyone breathed a sigh of relief. They were safe once more.

★ 1861 ★

Titus finished stacking some firewood next to the mess tent. He was glad he was done, for he could now relax and enjoy the rest of the evening.

As he walked towards his tent, he overheard a couple of Chaplains talking together about a new convert. Titus rolled his eyes as the first chaplain said, "I've been praying for this boy for years, and now, God has answered favorably to my prayers…"

"Answered favorably to my prayers," Titus mimicked under his breath. "I'm tired of people talking about prayer! 'God answered my prayer!' 'Prayer will help the matter!' Hmm!" He mulled over previous conversations about prayer, getting more irritated as he went.

Not paying attention to where he was going, Titus walked right into a man dressed in traveling attire, obviously not a soldier.

"Pardon me! I'm so sorry, sir-" he stopped suddenly. The man smiled brightly at him. "Jim!" It was his brother! They hugged each other tightly.

Jim stepped back to look at his younger brother. "Surely *one* battle can't change a boy into a man. I sure hope I found the right person. You are Titus Mallory, right?" he teased.

Titus playfully pushed his brother's shoulder. "Of course I am. When did you get out of prison?"

Jim had been arrested on false charges of trying to start an uprising against the United States in Maryland. The only thing he had done was print the truth about the conflict in the newspaper he published. When he wouldn't back down, his foes made up a story about his 'seditious' paper and life.

"They released me on Tuesday, so I guess that's six days ago. Missy and the children were staying with Mama and Papa, so I joined them until we can find a place of our own. It's not safe for us in Maryland anymore. We found out you were nearby, and they let me in to see you. Being a preacher helped."

Tuesday? Titus thought. *Wait a minute...that's when Tyler and the others were having their camp prayer meetings, praying that God would release him!* "How did you get out?"

"It was God that got me out. The judge saw through everything and released me. I knew people were praying for me, 'cause it was just too easy. I tell you one thing, Titus, prayer works."

Titus shifted uncomfortably. "Does everyone have to keep saying that?"

"Saying what?" asked Jim, a little bewildered by Titus' quick change of mood.

"Let's go over here where we can talk privately," he said, leading Jim over to a secluded part of the camp. They sat down on a fallen log.

Jim prayed silently for guidance in what to say.

"Now, Titus, will you please explain what you were talking about?" Titus was quiet, not sure how to answer and wishing he had not spoken his mind so quickly. He really didn't want to be in a bad mood while getting to visit with his brother he had missed seeing for such a long time.

Jim tried again. "Does it bother you to hear me talk about being in prison? The others told me how hard it was on you when I was sent away."

"No it's not that. I mean, it is partly, but a lot's been piling up. With you away…and the war… and everybody talkin' about prayer for this and prayin' for that…and answered prayers…and well…well, none of my prayers were answered. And I prayed every day after we heard you were arrested. I couldn't stand to watch mama crying, and we didn't know what was going to happen to Missy and the children.

"I really believed God would show them they were wrong and they would turn you loose. But as time went on, I didn't want to believe in anything. Especially prayer. So I joined up to try to make a difference."

"Have you made a difference?" Jim asked.

Titus shrugged. "Well, I'm not wasting my time on wondering if my prayers are gonna be answered. It seems everybody around me is getting prayers answered these days and if it works for them, then let 'em keep praying, but I'm done."

"Are you really? Don't you want peace in your heart? A peace that can go with you to battle? I had it in prison and joy too. Titus, you just need to get to know personally 'The One' you've been trying to pray to so your prayers can be prayed in the right spirit."

Titus fell silent again. Jim was praying he had not offended him. He remembered back to when he and Titus were young boys at home. Titus was the one that always had "a great plan" to solve any problem. He was a thinker. If Jim could just tap into those thoughts right now! He decided to just keep quiet a few more moments.

Silence didn't bother Titus; actually he welcomed it right now. He was reproaching himself again for answering his brother like he had. His mind and heart were in a battle. Did he really believe God wouldn't hear his prayers? Who was he really mad at anyway? Jim was out of prison now. Why couldn't he just be happy about that? Peace. Yes, that was it! Peace. There was no peace when he prayed. Could it be he was angry with the One he had been trying to pray to? Had he been giving God orders and commanding Him to follow them?

About this time, Jim slipped something into Titus' hand. Jim hadn't been sure when to give it to him. It was part of the reason he had come to the encampment in the first place.

Titus opened it up without looking up. It was a letter from his mother. His eyes fell on the opening words and he couldn't go any farther. Just seeing his mother's handwriting did something to this young boy's heart. It began:

Titus, my dear son, I'm praying for you…

Titus was turned away from Jim now; his head rested in his open hand. Mama's prayers were getting answered all these miles away. He looked at the letter again. The next line read:

…but more importantly, Jesus prays for you. It says so in the Bible. In John, it records a prayer He said for us, and in Romans it refers to Him as our intercessor. He even thinks about us! In Psalm 139:17, it says, "How precious also are thy thoughts unto me, O God! how great is the sum of them!"

Don't be angry with God, son, for our circumstances. Trust Him that He knows best what is best for us. Wisdom is brought about through trials. His ways are not our ways. He is perfect and He can see the whole picture. We can only see part of the story now.

There was more in the letter, but Titus' eyes kept going back to *Jesus prays for you*. He couldn't believe Jesus would pray for him as angry as he'd been lately. He knew he didn't deserve Jesus' prayers. But something about those words were stirring up things in Titus' heart.

He really wanted to be alone right now, but he also wanted to see his brother. He cleared his throat to try to speak to Jim, but Jim began first.

"Listen, Little Brother, I've got to run a couple more errands in the next town. How about I leave you with your letter and stop back by first thing in the morning?

Titus was relieved he didn't have to say much more. They gave each other a warm embrace and said their good-byes after arranging where to meet the next day.

After Jim rode away, Titus made his way back to his tent. He was glad the others had left. There was something he needed to do. He reached under his pillow and brought out an old New Testament his mother had sent with him when he joined up.

She had carefully marked verses in it before giving it to him and asked him to read it daily. He had meant to. He had tried to. But his weak attempts fell by the wayside and soon he was only keeping his Bible with him as a remembrance of his mother and not as a 'help' as she had meant it to be.

But now, he knew he needed that 'help.' He took the testament and walked quickly back to where he had said goodbye to Jim. In the light that was left he began to read those marked verses.

Romans 3:23, For all have sinned, and come short of the glory of God;

Romans 5:12, Wherefore, as by one man sin entered into the world, and death by sin; and so death passed upon all men, for that all have sinned:

Romans 6:23, For the wages of sin is death; but the gift of God is eternal life through Jesus Christ our Lord.

Romans 5:8, But God commendeth his love toward us, in that, while we were yet sinners, Christ died for us.

Romans 10:9-10,13, That if thou shalt confess with thy mouth the Lord Jesus, and shalt believe in thine heart that God hath raised him from the dead, thou shalt be saved. For with the heart man believeth unto righteousness; and with the mouth confession is made unto salvation. ¹³For whosoever shall call upon the name of the Lord shall be saved.

The prayers had worked, that heart was ready, the struggle was over. Titus fully surrendered his heart to the Lord. Surrendered all. When he replaced his New Testament in its place that night and laid his head down on his pillow, he was a new soldier…a soldier in the Lord's Army!

★1861★

Chapter 24

★

That Time of Year

Trust in the LORD with all thine heart; and lean not unto thine own understanding.
Psalm 3:5

Dixie picked up her book of war memorabilia she had started. It had filled quickly with all the events of the past year. She read some of the old articles then turned to the more recent ones.

On the 1st of November, General Winfield Scott [21] resigned as commander in chief of the Union armies. He was replaced by George McClellan[22]. On the 7th, the Confederates inflicted a tactical defeat on Gen. Grant at Belmont, Missouri. The 8th sent Southerners and British into a fit of indignation.

---

[21] Known as "Old Fuss 'n Feathers," Gen. Scott received Robert E. Lee's resignation in April.
[22] "Little Mac" became one of the most beloved generals of the Union Army, even if he wasn't the best. It was said he could win any battle, if waged on paper.

U.S. Captain Charles Wilkes[23] took two Confederate envoys[24] captive off the British mail ship *Trent*. The men were James M. Mason (no kin to our Masons!) and John Slidell.

Dixie found out that on the 30th of November, the British Government was demanding the release of Mr. James Mason and Mr. John Slidell and they insisted on an apology for their seizure. Things were starting to get interesting!

Meanwhile Michael was in the boys' room once again reading Richard's most recent letter.

Dear Family,

Seth and I are doing fine, and we hope the same is true of y'all. Please pray for Maxwell Houston, one of our drummer boys. He had a 'bullet meet bone' situation and...well anyway, he can't walk anymore. He ain't taking it too well. We really need another drummer, that way we can have him trained and ready for next spring...

Michael stared out the window. He knew he could easily fill that spot. He and Carter played drummer boys all the time. They both could do a fairly good drum roll.

Michael prayed about the possibility ever since he first read the letter. He knew his mother wouldn't be keen on the idea, but he couldn't shake the thought. After all, he was thirteen now. Maybe God could use him, just like he used David in the Bible...

He continued reading the letter.

...Oh, by the way, on the 30th of September, we actually got to see President Davis! He was in our

---

[23] Captain of the U.S.S. *San Jacinto*. Best known for his seizure of the two Confederate envoys.
[24] John Mason is a former U.S. Senator and Confederate Commissioner to England. John Slidell is a Confederate Commissioner to France.

area for some meeting, I think, and we saw him at the train station. He looked rather thin and tired. Must be the stress of running a nation.

You may already know this, but General Jackson has been promoted again, this time to Major General[25]! We have a new brigade commander, Richard Garnett[26]. He's alright, but he's not Gen. Jackson. I hope we will soon be reunited with his army in Winchester. We're still under his command, but we're not there with him...oh well.

Tyler still leads prayer meetings every week here in camp, which are very encouraging. He's still nervous about it, but he seems a little more confident when he speaks. Chaplain thinks he should get up a short devotion for next week, so we'll see how that goes! He's been stuck to his Bible practically every spare moment he has!

We've noticed a big change in Titus lately. He comes to services regularly and doesn't seem irritated when we're talking about the sermons around him. He actually seems interested now.

Got a letter from Nate Bowers last week. He says he's back in school and getting along well with the help of his crutches.

He informed us that David is still working at a hospital in Richmond. Nate says David was baptized

---

[25] When promoted to Brig. General, Jackson was transferred to Winchester, Va. His beloved brigade rejoined him later that fall.
[26] Brig. Gen. Garnett will later be relieved of his command by Gen. Jackson for disobeying orders in 1862.

and joined their church when they got home this summer...

★1861★

In early December, Michael entered Dixie's room and found her with books scattered all over her bed.

"What's all this stuff?" Michael asked as he came to sit next to her.

Dixie looked up from the volume she was reading. "Huh? Oh, it's a bunch of books of family history. I found them in the attic. It's really interesting. This book is a journal written by Mary Mason. It was written from 1620-1623. It says that the original Masons were Germans that had been raised in England and came to Massachusetts. The Leonard family was German as well and had settled in England and left for America aboard the same boat as the Masons. They-"

"Whoa, wait. Who are the Leonards?" Michael asked.

"Oh, sorry. Mary's maiden name was Leonard. She married Justice Mason in 1622. Then they emigrated to North Carolina in the late 1600's. The Leonard children were orphans when they came to America and there were at least six of them counting Mary. After Mary and Justice got married, they took in all of Mary's siblings, the youngest being four years old at the time.

"And this journal says that Mary and Justice had twelve children of their own!" she finished, holding up another journal.

"Whew! Now that must have been somethin'!" Michael said. "And during that time they founded Four Tree Springs, too?"

"Yep, sure did. It's been the home to our families ever since. Can you imagine the size of their family vegetable garden?" Dixie asked.

"Probably about the size of one our cotton fields!" Michael suggested. "Hey, look, it's snowing!" They hurried over to the window for a better look.

"I hope it sticks! Dixie said excitedly. They hardly ever got snow. Michael grinned, albeit sleepily. After looking out the window a few more minutes, they bade each other goodnight and headed for bed.

★1861★

That first snow had been disappointing; barely a dusting. But later that month, Dixie and Michael watched as the first *real* snow fell, lightly covering the ground and barn. "Children, eat your breakfast and quit staring out the window!" Mrs. Bradley said smiling. "This is the last day of school before the holidays! Christmas and the New Year are just around the corner!"

"Sorry," Michael said, taking his seat at the table. "It's just that it don't snow that often."

Mama laughed. "You would love it in Pennsylvania during the winter. I've seen enough snow to last me a lifetime!"

A knock came at the kitchen door. Dixie hurried to open it. "Oh, Aunt Lou! Come on in! Mama, Aunt Lou's here." Mr. and Mrs. Roberts had requested that the children refer to them as Uncle Will and Aunt Lou, which they were more used to.

Aunt Lou entered the kitchen with the youngest two children. "I'm here and ready to help you and Miz Bradley wid de baking, Miz Mason."

Mama came around the corner. "Oh, good. It'll be nice to have y'all's company today.

"Well, a lady in your condition don't need to be working too hard," Aunt Lou said with a twinkle in her eye.

Mama laughed. "I still have a few months before my family expands, and you're in the same boat!"

Dixie laughed as the two women teased each other. She was excited about the coming sibling. Their last sibling had taken sick and died when Michael was little. Oh, how they were praying this baby would be healthy.

They hurried to finish and get ready for school. It was mid-December, and they were going to ride on horseback to school. They quickly went out to the barn to saddle Confederate and Lady. Lady's foals were five months old and frisky. Blue nipped at Dixie's dress as she passed his stall. She playfully swatted at him which sent him into an excited little fit of bucking. Dixie laughed and finished bridling Confederate.

Michael led Lady out of the large stall. Gray protested loudly, but Lady seemed undisturbed. Before long they were on their way to the schoolhouse. "I feel like George Washington[27] at Valley Forge in 1777. They lost many men that year," Michael said as his teeth began to chatter.

Dixie wrapped her cloak tighter around her shoulders. "Yeah, but don't forget, the Patriots won the war in the end. And George Washington became the first President of the United States! I'm sure he would be angry if he saw what was going on less than 100 years later. I think he would be a Confederate. Remember, Papa said that the Yankees are acting like the British and George Washington was against the British! The cold didn't stop the Patriots then, so it won't stop us now. We serve the same God Mr. Washington did."

Michael nodded in agreement, pulled his scarf off and rewrapped it. Dixie had made it for him for his birthday. It hadn't come too soon!

"I love this time of year," Dixie said. "We get to celebrate Jesus' birthday, but it'll be different celebrating it without Richard and Seth." She frowned. How she wished the whole family could be together for Christmas. It just wouldn't be the same.

---

[27] First President of the United States.

Chapter 25

★

Christmas Apart

Therefore the Lord himself shall give you a sign; Behold, a virgin shall conceive, and bear a son, and shall call his name Immanuel.
Isaiah 7:14

Christmas Day after breakfast, Silas skimmed over an old newspaper while he waited for the rest of the family to join him in the sitting room. The cover story was about the release of James Mason and John Slidell. The article stated that U.S. Secretary of State, William Seward[28] had acknowledged the error in their seizure and the British had received an apology.

It also announced the birth of William Howell Davis[29] on December 6th. The whole Confederacy felt enthralled by the birth of the President and First Lady's baby.

---

[28] U.S. Secretary of State and former governor of New York. He served as the Secretary of State from March of 1861- March of 1869.
[29] This President's child was quite the morale booster to the Confederacy.

Dixie entered the room, followed shortly by Mama. Silas smiled as he heard Michael bounding down the stairs. He soon joined them.

As soon as he was seated, Papa said, "I have a very special Christmas present for us." He pulled a letter from his vest pocket. Dixie squealed. A letter from the boys!

Dear Family,

Merry Christmas and Happy New Year! Greetings from the 2nd Virginia Regiment encampment! We hope this letter finds everyone in good health and having a wonderful time with the rest of the Mason clan!

Things in camp are going slow. Glad for a time of no hostilities! Can you imagine fighting in the winter? That would be very difficult!

In answer to Michael's question, I (Seth) have decided to name the colts Stonewall (the grey one) and Bull Run (the blue one). I couldn't name a blue colt Manassas, though Richard and Tyler have given me no end of teasing for the "unpatriotic" name. I told them I wasn't going with a Yankee name; they didn't name Bull Run creek, and that is where the colt's name was taken from. I thought Mama would like it that the colts were named for the events that took place the day they were born.

We were right about Titus Mallory being different somehow these days. It came out in a conversation recently. His words were "...I decided to surrender one big battle so I could get on better with this one." He's really changed.

I guess Mama and Papa cooked Christmas breakfast together like they usually do, since the Bradleys are probably gone for the holidays already. Some things never change. Wish more things would stay the same...

...Looking forward to the day we will all be together again! Give everyone our best regards. We love y'all!

Love,
Richard and Seth

★ 1861 ★

"I don't understand why Jeremiah hasn't written me," Cornelia Calling said, pacing the sitting room. "I hope nothing's happened to him."

These words were directed to her younger brother, André. The careless fourteen year old shrugged. "I'm sure he's fine, sis. Probably too busy running from our soldiers to write."

Cornelia frowned. It was Christmas day and she longed for some word from her beloved older brother. "Nobody's running from anyone. The armies have dug in for the winter and you know that! Something must have happened, or he would certainly have-"

"Miss Cornelia?" one of the servants said, stepping into the room. "A letter for you."

"Jeremiah! Oh, thank you, Ethel." She eagerly snatched the letter and opened it, glancing at the address on the front. She stopped. "This isn't his handwriting."

André rolled his eyes. "Maybe he's been dreadfully wounded and can't write his dying words to you himself," he said sarcastically.

Cornelia looked at him sharply. "Don't talk like that! That's horrible to even imagine!" She stood and left the room, heading for the privacy of her bedroom. André's words had frightened her. *Who else would be writing me from Virginia? Why else than to tell me that Jeremy was either sick or...*

She entered her room and closed the door. Taking a deep breath, she removed the letter from the envelope.

Miss Cornelia Calling,

You may not remember me, but I'm your former neighbor, Alvin Willis, a friend of Jeremy's. He shared some of your letter with me, which led to this letter being sent to you. I felt you should know some things about him he may not tell you himself.

He's a good influence on me and the other boys in camp. He's a good friend and speaks of y'all often with deep love for y'all. He misses y'all a lot...

...A few months ago, he had an encounter with the enemy. We were rejoining our brigade and a Union picket spotted him and a friend who were hunting up some fresh meat. A chase followed, complete with bloodhounds.

Cornelia gasped. Her face flushed with indignation. *Her* soldiers had turned bloodhounds loose on *her* brother? Why? How she hated war! She continued reading.

At one point, he and his friend knew they needed to escape, but a trail needed to be left for the dogs to follow. Jeremy put his own life in danger and helped his friend escape, resulting in his being caught by the dogs and the northern soldiers.

Your brother is very selfless, Miss Cornelia. He didn't know what the enemy planned to do with him, but he chose to be captured rather than let his friend be hurt. He's a good man.

I'm happy to let you know he is now back in camp with us, safe and sound. I don't know if he's written a response to your letter, but I do know this: Jeremy is no quitter. I assure you he has prayed over your pleas for him to come home, but I believe he will not leave his post until this conflict is over…

…He doesn't know I'm writing this to you. Please let your family know that if Jeremy has changed at all, it is only for the better. His love for y'all has not wavered and I hope for all of y'all to be reconciled and at peace with each other.

Respectfully,
Pvt. Alvin Willis, C.S. Army

Tears slid down Cornelia's cheeks. *He's going to stay with his army,* she thought, her heart breaking from the reality. *Papa won't let him come home!* She let the letter fall to the floor as she turned her face into her pillow and wept.

Knock, knock.

Cornelia tried to gain her composure as her father entered the room. "André told me you had a letter from an unknown source. Care to share, darling? Is this what has my little girl in tears?"

Cornelia nodded as her father retrieved the pages from the floor. She put them back in order and he began to read. She watched his face carefully. She was having trouble reading him. He frowned at first, then his countenance softened, then the frown returned.

He mumbled something Cornelia couldn't quite understand, but she thought he said something about cowardice and heroics not mixing in one body. "He seems to have made his choice, dear. I'll take the letter for now."

Cornelia nodded as he kissed her cheek and left the room. Her door had scarcely closed before her tears had returned. What a dreadful, ugly Christmas this had been for her.

★ 1861 ★

Richard and Seth sat at their camp fire with their fellow soldiers enjoying a Christmas ration of coffee. A fiddler was playing a lively Christmas tune nearby, and the snow had stopped for the moment. The boys were grateful for the warm scarves that had been sent to them in the mail.

"You're awful quiet, Seth," Tyler commented. "What ya' thinking about?"

"Christmas back home. Papa and Mama and the others are probably at Christmas services in town right now." He wore a far off look as he rubbed the growing beard on his chin. "Dixie's probably gonna sing a duet with Lana tonight."

Richard nodded. "Yep, and they had dinner at Paw-Paw and Maw-Maw's yesterday. I wonder how many of the family members were able to come in for Christmas."

"Think they got our letter in time for today?" Seth asked.

Richard shrugged. "Maybe so. Guess we'll know in a few weeks. What I wouldn't give to be home right now!"

The others voiced their agreement and shared memories of past Christmases and loved ones at home.

Seth gazed up at the stars. He smiled as he thought that his family would soon be looking at those same stars when church let out. He thought over the past year…so much had happened…so much had changed. He'd experienced a change of allegiances, joined a fledgling army, and watched as his commander had led a legendary stand in the first major conflict of the war.

Then he thought of the things he'd missed out on; watching as Michael learned how to help Papa around Shady Grove Plantation…watching Dixie change from a young girl to a young lady right under his nose…eating Maw-Maw's pumpkin pie…hearing Papa reading the Christmas story, and listening to Mama and Papa telling about Christmas as children.

It had been a full year and a busy one. *What will next year hold?* he wondered. Would the war end? Could they return home in peace and safety?

Seth closed his eyes. *It'll be over next year,* he assured himself. *It'll all be over…and we can go home and be together again…*

A Personal Touch

<u>Shady Grove:</u> The name for the Shady Grove Plantation came from what we call our wooded area next to our house. Shady Grove is where we go for relaxation and recreation.

<u>The Cats:</u> We really do have a cat named Peek-a-boo and the kittens are based on cats we have owned at one time or another.

<u>Christmas Breakfast:</u> My parents make breakfast together on Christmas day every year. That's a tradition they started since before I can remember!

You have definitely seen some similarities between my characters and my family members here and there. Strong southern heritage and loyalty runs in our veins.

★1861★

My Testimony

In September 2001, 9-11 took place. I was five years old, and I remember people talking about the planes flying into the Twin Towers. I didn't understand what was going on, but it scared me. When I heard about all those people dying, it set me to thinking about where I would go after I died.

On July 3rd, 2002, when I was six, my sister Gera and I were playing David and Goliath in our backyard. Dad was grilling in preparation for America's birthday the following day. Different things from sermons I'd heard came to my mind, and I began asking dad some questions. To be honest, I don't remember what the exact questions were, but I do remember that they had to do with Salvation.

Dad answered my questions to my satisfaction, and I went back to play, but the conviction of the Holy Spirit compelled me to settle the question of my eternity that day. I knelt next to my mom's flower garden and asked the Lord to forgive me of my sins and save me. I have never regretted that decision.

My interest in history began in fourth grade when I did a course on the U.S. Presidents. I was captivated by the details and wanted to know more. My parents kept me supplied with books and courses on different parts of history over the next few years. The Civil War time era became my favorite topic to study.

By the time I was 14 I had read a number of books on the Civil War and was irritated by the misinformation I kept seeing concerning the cause of the war. I expressed this to my sister and told her I just wanted to read the truth. Her reply? "Write your own books." I don't think she knew I would take her seriously. After several failed attempts at a beginning, I figured out what I wanted. So in January of 2011, I began writing, *The Land of Cotton*.

During this time my mom encouraged me not to just write for fun and myself, but to give my hobby to the Lord and attempt publishing. I was scared, but I agreed. Later, the Lord used a man at the church I grew up in to bless me by buying me a laptop, printer and all the extras! My writing and typing took on new meaning then.

In December of 2011, *The Land of Cotton* was completed!...or so I thought. Well, I revamped my book, had Gera and others read it, corrected errors, made more changes, etc. I continued writing the *Battle for Heritage Series*.

I went on to finish the series in 2014, five books in all. That year I got up the courage to have mom read my first book. She liked it but knew it needed more work. We had no idea how much work it would need! More editing, eliminating, adding, proofing, reading, researching, praying, typing, long nights, cups of hot chocolate and talking went into this book. At last, we added the final polishing touches. Off to the proofers! Then to the printers! And now, you're holding it in your hands!

But none of this would be possible if I hadn't yielded to the Holy Spirit and asked Jesus to save me. I could have become like David and Titus in the story, lost and without hope. Or perhaps I would have become like Constance Angelica, ill and sour. But for the grace of God, that could be me…but is that you?

All you must do is believe that Jesus is the Son of God, that He died on the cross, was buried, and rose again on the third day. Ask Him to forgive you of your sins and to take you to heaven when you die.

Or are you a follower of Christ, but like Tyler, asleep to the work of God and His will for your life? Are you living to serve Him? If not, I challenge you now to do as Tyler did. Dedicate your life to the Lord and move forward in your walk with the Lord. Serve Him in all things and allow Him to do great things through you. (Romans 12:1-2)

This book is not just about getting your history straight, though that is one of its goals. This book is about making sure you know Jesus Christ as your Savior and serving Him with your whole life. I pray this book has been a help to you.

May God Bless You!
Writing for HIM,

Ryana Lynn Miller

The Story Continues...

Our Heritage to Save
1862
Our Fight For Freedom

Book 2 in the Battle for Heritage Series

So, what does 1862 hold for the Mason family? What will the new baby be? Another brother, or will Dixie finally get a sister? What about Michael's interest in being a drummer boy? What will Richard and Seth face as the war continues?

These and other questions are answered in *Our Heritage to Save*, and new questions offer themselves for consideration. Learn about the battles of Shiloh, Antietam, Fredericksburg and more in the sequel to *The Land of Cotton*. Learn the truth about a document you may not have considered before. And learn about an incident in Missouri that will blow your mind. Don't miss *Our Heritage to Save*, a celebration of the sacrifice of the brave men and women of the 19th century!

Please tune in...

The Fundamental Broadcasting Network
fbnradio.com
A local church ministry of Grace Baptist Church
in Newport, North Carolina

FBN offers:
- ✓ King James only Preaching
- ✓ Conservative Christian Music
- ✓ Short Devotionals
- ✓ Dramatizations and Cantatas
- ✓ Preachers and Singers of the Past and Present and much, much more!

You won't have to worry about something inappropriate coming into your home with this radio station! We have been heard in all 50 states and in over 218 countries and territories! We also have a children's site, fbnkids.com!

How Can You Listen?
- ✓ By Internet: fbnradio.com
- ✓ By Free Apps for Apple and Android devices
- ✓ Livestream By Phone: 712-432-4370
- ✓ By Radio: Check our Website for a list of all of our 40+ stations and see if we have one in your area, or write/call FBN for a free program guide.

520 Roberts Rd.
Newport, NC 28570
252-223-4600

We Would Love to Hear From You!